two of their agents trailing the drug shipments. The first was killed in Panama City, Florida, The other in Houston, Texas. That is when they called the Director of Drug Operations, the man in charge in Colombia, Paul Bozares. That is why Shelby was now sitting on her heals in the middle of the jungle, sweating like a pig, waiting for the call from America. Shelby thought back three days ago to another phone call she received.

Chapter 3

Shelby received the call at three-thirty in the morning while on a stake out for the mule she was sure would be coming down the trail. Her team had worked for weeks sitting up this sting and tonight was to be the payoff. This mule was no ordinary mule; he was the cousin of the drug lord in that area. Shelby knew when they captured him with all the drugs and they let him know how many years he would be serving in a Colombia jail that he would start talking. So she was mad as hell when the phone call from her superior told her to drop the surveillance and catch the next plane to headquarters and a meeting with the Director.

Twelve hours later she was climbing the steps to the federal building in Bogota where the Director had his office and she was still mad. It never once crossed her mind, as it would for most agents, to be worried about why the Director wanted to see her, she didn't care. The only thing on her mind was to let someone know how pissed off she was that all the work she and her team had done for the last four months was now down the drain.

Shelby checked her image in the hall mirror before stopping at the receptionist desk. Staring back at her was a 31-year-old woman with short jet-black hair and startling black eyes. She looked up and down her five foot seven inch figure and the pantsuit she had hastily iron that morning. Then at the figure that always turned the heads of every male she passed. Even the woman gave a second look before turning away in envy. Satisfied that everything was in place she strolled to the receptionist's desk and flashed her I.D. without saying a word. The receptionist glanced at her I.D. leaned over and touched a small green button.

"Agent Cruse to see you Director."

"Send her in please." Came the reply.

"Second door to your right down the hall, Agent Cruse." She said as she pointed in the direction for Shelby to go.

Without a thank you or a nod Shelby turned and walked in the direction pointed out to her. The cold eyes of the receptionist followed her until she saw her, without knocking, open the second door on her right and walk in as if she owned the place. The room was devoid of furniture, not a single chair, not even a window. "Place your palm on the wall plate please, Agent Cruse." Came the voice from the walls. When she did as she was instructed the wall in front of her slid open revealing an elevator large enough for two to three people only. Once she stepped inside she saw that there were no buttons but before she could comment the door slid shut and the elevator shot downward so fast she felt her stomach trying to reach her throat. Shelby calculated she had gone at least ten stories down when the door opened to two burly men, each carrying side arms.

"Open you jacket please Agent Cruse." The shorter one said as he slid his hands over her inside jacket and removed the small gun that she carried. "Please step behind the screen and do not move please." The second man said as he motioned for her to step where he had indicated. Shelby knew what was coming next; it was one of those new fancy machines that had Superman's ex-ray eyes. Her belief was proven when she looked at her reflection on the glass wall and saw herself in all her glory. By the time she looked at the two men they had already turned their backs to her and was filling out their report, so much for thinking they would get a big charge at looking at her body, Shelby thought. Although that never happened very many times in her life her respect went up a notch for both men. "Please use the door on your left Agent Cruse." The shorter man said as he smiled at her.

Shelby strolled to the door and without hesitation opened it and walked into the room. Although there were no windows in the room it looked and felt like the outdoors. Half the room had large plants growing from floor to ceiling and a wonderful soothing waterfall was cascading down from one corner of the room and splashed into a rather large pond for the size of the room. Sitting behind a very large oak desk was Paul Gozares, Director of Drug Operations for Columbia. He was not looking up. His massive built looked to big for the chair he was setting in and the large rough hands were flipping pages from the folder on his desk. Shelby stood three feet in front of the desk and waited, he knew she was here she was not going to be the one to make the first move. She watched his eyes as they scanned the papers; clear blue eyes that she could tell missed nothing. As his eyes left the pages and lifted to meet her eyes Shelby at that instance realized what he had been scanning. It was her file. Their eyes locked for full two seconds before the Director spoke.

"Please be seated Agent Cruse." The Director motioned for her to be seated in the middle chair of the three in front of his desk, the one directly in front of him. Shelby couldn't hold her tongue any longer.

"I don't know what is so important Director Gozares that you had me pulled from a stakeout in which my team had worked more than four months sitting up. Surely it could have waited another day before----" His head and eyes had been down reading the remainder of her file when she began to speak. His eyes flashed and with a short quick flick of his hand the message came across loud and clear to her. Keep your mouth

The Money Trail

by

CHICK LUNG

authorHOUSE®

AuthorHouse™
1663 Liberty Drive, Suite 200
Bloomington, IN 47403
www.authorhouse.com
Phone: 1-800-839-8640

First published by AuthorHouse 1/21/2008

ISBN: 978-1-4343-5855-4 (sc)

*Printed in the United States of America
Bloomington, Indiana*

This book is printed on acid-free paper.

Chapter 1

Alex Bell took the stairs three at a time from the sixth floor conference room. He had to get out, he had to get fresh air or puke all over the documents his partner, Chuck Witt, had laid before him. Alex felt faint, sweat soaked his suit, and even his socks were wet. He grabbed hard the cold metal railing as he descended to the first floor. Fumbling for his handkerchief he finally yanked it out and mopped his face and neck. Alex wasn't sure he would make the revolving front door before his insides gushed up and spilled out onto the glass like marble floor. And he was right; he never made the door before the foul burning liquid squirted between his clinched teeth and lips.

With one hand holding the handkerchief to his mouth Alex ran past the startled morning watchman through the revolving door into the sunshine. Alex reached the Bench Park close to the tree that the people of Oklahoma had named The Survival Tree. When the Rider rental truck blasted half the Federal Murrah Building away this lone tree stood proud and tall against the carnage surrounding it. The heat was so hot it melted the tires on every vehicle parked near and the asphalt surrounding the tree flowed like heavy molasses for over fifty feet. And yet this tree stood and in a few weeks began to produce leaves, showing the world that among the carnage natures will to survive was strong. With the cool April breeze on his face Alex took long deep breaths until his insides calmed down enough for him to try and think clearly. Alex looked up at the tree and than at his watch, the time was 9:02 A.M., the date was April 19, 2007. *My God he thought, twice on the same date and time! Twelve years ago at this exact time I was in my office in the Journal Records Building directly across from the Murrah building looking out the window at a yellow Rider rental truck parked next to the building.* Alex's mind wondered back to that awful moment when the Murrah building exploded sending him flying backwards against the opposite wall of his office. Small pieces of window glass sliced his face and arms to ribbons. For two years he had one surgery after another and today you would have to look hard to see the tiny scars dotting his face. And now this, on the same date?

Chuck Witt, my partner and friend for the last 22 years, just gutted my life. How could a friend or even a partner deliberately do such a thing; we went to college together, took most of the same classes and upon graduation started our own small company. We built our dream working eighteen-hour days for ten years before it took off. Now we were suppose to be set for life with the company growing bigger every year and major corporations calling on a weekly basis, throwing more money then we ever dreamed possible, trying to buy us out.

Chapter 2

Shelby squatted with her rear only inches from the damp leaves covering the ground for more than four hours, seldom taking the binoculars from her eyes as she watched the shinny white house that covered half of the small plateau over looking the village below. Shelby eased one leg straight out while still squatting on the other to ease the stiffness and then repeated the motion with the other leg. Shelby knew if it had been necessary for her not to move it would not have been a problem. She had squatted in this position many times before with instructions not to move a muscle, to become invisible to anything watching, both man and beast. As a nine-year old she squatted for twelve hours at a time, not moving a muscle, knowing she would be beaten or starved if she did. The leather holster of her M11/9 Cobray that was attached to her hip brushed against leaves lying on the ground. The second gun, a Micro Uzis, was strapped to the middle of her back.

Twenty-seven huts, none made with anything resembling brick, were scattered in the few man made clearings below. Shelby had not counted them after she made her way through the thick jungle to the spot she was now occupying. There had been no need too she knew every inch of the ground around this wretched and ugly small place. She had last looked down from this exact spot twenty-two years ago when she was 9 years old and running from the terror she had just witnessed in the big house on the plateau. Things had not changed, the village was still nothing but shacks made of sticks and leaves and mud. Looking at one particular house the memories came flooding back of a happy time when she was very young. But what child knows of the world around her other than her father and mother and the jungle clearing to play in. The darkness and pain had not yet entered her small mind and Shelby allowed a small smile to cross her face as she watched herself running after the monkey and her baby. It was a game not only to her but to the mother monkey as Shelby darted one way and than another as she tried to get close. And each time she got within a certain distance the monkey with her baby hanging on tight would jump to a tree and scamper up ten to twenty feet before stopping and looking down at the base of the tree where Shelby stood looking up.

If anyone had witness this scene they would have sworn the small girl was talking to the monkey. First the monkey would let out a loud screech and the small girl would mimic her perfect. This went on for minutes before one or the other would stop and then the other would stop and rest. Sometimes one or the other would start up again and they would repeat the game until the monkey turned her attention to her baby and forgot the human creature below her. Shelby was five years old when the game came to a dramatic stop one hot afternoon. She had just chased the monkey back up the tree for the third time that day and was beginning to talk to her and her baby when she heard a large crack, like a big limb had been broken. It took her child's mind a few nano seconds before what her eyes registered reached her brain and every thing was in slow motion as she watched the mother monkey's head explode as she slowly fell from the tree still holding the baby in her arm.

Shelby turned to her left and saw the big man, she knew his name was Hernando Kling, holding a large ugly gun and he was smiling. "Take the meat little one and have your mother cook it for you," he laughed. All Shelby could see was the evil smile and the thick white scare running from the corner of his left eye to the base of his face as she picked up a stick and ran for him screaming as fast as she could. She swung the stick as hard as she could against the man's leg. He only laughed as he reached out a large hand and hit her on the side of her face, knocking her rolling in the dust and mud. Shelby knew he was one of the guards from the big house and she cried in silence as she watched him climb the hill, whistling a popular tune of the time.

Squatting, Shelby felt the hot tears running down her face as she caressed the handle of the M11/9 Cobray. She knew if the man was in front of her right then she would have cut him in half with the sixty rounds that would spit out in the first three seconds after pulling the trigger. But he was not who she was watching for, he was just a small fish, she was after the big one, the Barracuda of the house. His name was Hector King and he was the lord of the jungle in this area and had been for more than forty years.

Adjusting the phone plug in her ear Shelby moved the controls on the small black box on the ground beside her. The satellite phone call would be made in five minutes from Houston to the remote jungle of Colombia, to the big house on the plateau she now had her glasses on. Any conversation going into or out of the house would be picked up by her and recorded by the black box. The United States Drug Enforcement Agency wanted very badly to know when the big shipment was coming. Twice before they thought they had made a bust only to be confused, not knowing what happened to the shipment or even if the shipment had ever left Colombia. But Hector King had committed the Cardinal Sin against the United States Drug Enforcement Agency. He had ordered the killing of shut until I ask you to speak. Shelby's back went ridged and her mouth clamp shut as he continued to look into her eyes. When he saw she had gotten his message he turned her file back to the beginning and began to read out loud.

Chapter 4

"Shelby Cruse, 31 years old, born outside Mitu in a small village, date of birth and location never verified, presumed area bordering the country of Brazil. Raised as an orphan at the age of ten by the Bazzaren family. Bazzaren family stated you were found wondering half starved at the edge of the jungle close to their village. Found you had zero school education and was placed in lowest grade. School authorities, after one year of schooling, placed you in advance studies, I.Q. test came back off the charts. Finished high school at fourteen completed all twelve grades in four years and your Bachelor of Science at sixteen. Colombia's Secretary of Education funded your further education to any university requested. You chose Yale in the United States for your PHD. Which you finished at nineteen." Director Gozares pauses and looked at Shelby before focusing his eyes back on her folder.

"Requested and received permission to attend Harvard Law School. Received your law degree at 22 and requested permission to attend the elite F.B.I. Academy. Colombia was required to pull in some very heavy favors to get you accepted. Finished at the top of your class, as I might add, you have at every school you have ever attended. All the reports state you have an IQ in the genius range."

"After graduating from the F.B.I. Academy, which offered you a job as one of their agents and you turned down, you applied for a position with this department and began working undercover immediately. That was at your request, to be involved with anything to do with drug smuggling. In two years you were responsible for more arrest than all the rest of your department combined. Assigned as special agent to the elite drug force under Captain Ruiz. In the five years you have been assigned to Captain Ruiz his forces have arrested or killed more drug traffickers then the total for the whole country for more than ten years. Captain Ruiz, in an extremely glowing report on you, has stated if he had just ten more like you that he could eliminate the other ninety on his force. Captain Ruiz also states you have refused three promotions, the last one to be his deputy." Shelby kept her face in a neutral position, he wasn't telling her anything she didn't know, the question going through her mind was, why was he bringing all this up?

"Let's see Agent Cruse, a couple of miscellaneous things at the end here are interesting. You hold a fourth degree black belt, and used that skill to kill a drug dealer with one blow to his windpipe when he tried to stab you with a hidden knife he had in his boot when you and another agent arrested him. The other agent reported it was the quickest most efficient kill he had ever witnessed. And than he did something interesting Agent Cruse, he underlined in red the next sentence. After Agent Cruse verified the man was dead no emotion on her part was shown nor did she make any excuse that the kind of force she used was necessary, in fact seconds afterwards it was as if the incident had never happened." The Director paused to look at Shelby again and the only thing he got were two dark black eyes staring defiantly back at him.

You were awarded the highest metal the Colombia Government bestows on a citizen when you and Captain Ruiz entered a house you though held a drug supplier and stumbled across the kidnapped wife of the Governor of Buenaventura that half of the Colombia army was hunting for. In hand to hand fighting, at which time you were stabbed in the thigh and twice in the back, you disabled two men guarding the Governors wife. Advancing into the next room Captain Ruiz and you encountered three armed men. Captain Ruiz shot one man dead before being shot three times and being disabled. His report stated before either man could turn their guns on you that you had advanced within striking distance with your weapons holstered. Your first blow caught the tip of the first mans nose and drove it into his brain and your second blow entered the other mans solar plexus and ruptured his heart. All while severely injured Agent Cruse! If I put some Krypton in front of you would you faint or would all you powers be gone Agent Cruse?"

"I beg your pardon Sir!"

"Never mind Agent Cruse, that was just an inside joke we have around here." The Director said, as he kept his eyes on her for any kind of reaction, when he got none he continued.

"You also speak three languages fluently other than your native tongue, French, English and Russia."

"Four."

"Four what?"

"You said I speak three other languages Sir, I speak four, the other is Chinese, five different dialectics of Chinese." The Director looked at Shelby without smiling before he again spoke.

"Why are you doing this Agent Cruse? Why are you putting your life on the line every day and why are you satisfied with the small amount of money you draw as a salary when you could go to the business world and make a hundred times as much?"

"I like my work Director Gozares."

"And alarm bells go off in my head Agent Cruse when I go through your file. You're a loner; you have no boyfriends or girlfriends that I can see. No one ever comes to your apartment, not even to share a dinner with you. It shows you took a month vacation in the fall when you were sixteen before attending Yale, no record of where you went. You took another month's vacation between your junior and senior year at Harvard Law School when you were twenty-one, again no record of where you went. You took a third vacation that was again one month long while working for us at the age of twenty-six, again no record of where you went. That strike's me as strange Agent Cruse, you don't take normal vacations like everyone else and when you do take one it's a month long and no one knows where you go! If you keep to that pattern Agent Cruse it seems you will be requesting another month vacation to some unknown destination in a few months. What is it Cruse, do you need your batteries recharged only once every five years?" When the Director got no response he turned his attention back to the file.

"You get along with your fellow workers, both male and female, at lease until they make a mistake in the field, then you refuse to ever, and I mean ever, work with them in the field again. Not even when you were ordered to I might add. Your skill at killing hand to hand is unmatched and your detachment afterwards is frightening. There is no remorse, no sadness or sorrow, no second guessing of what happened, it had to be done and you did it as efficient and as precise as a skilled surgeon and you never bring the subject up after your report has been submitted. It's as if it was a small requirement of your job and nothing to have feelings about one way or the other, so I keep coming back to the question, why?"

"Why what Director! Why am I good at my job? I like my job and I do it the best I can, I study hard and while some of the other agents are home with their wives and husbands I've got my nose in a book or a report, that is the only way you can stay on top. One false move while you're in the field, one small detail overlooked or one you forgot to look up or study and the next thing that happens is they will be picking up your body in a body bag. I've seen it Director, there were some very good agents I had to zip the body bag on because they forgot one small thing or left one extra thing out for someone to see. It's a deadly game we play Director and it's one of death when you fail as those agents did. I do not intend to be the one they zip the body bag over because of an error by me. I cannot control the errors of others but I can make sure that no errors are made by me."

"Now I'm tired of this game Director, you had me pulled from a job that took months to set up, I deserve an explanation to that or at lease please get to the point of why I am here." Director Cozares only nodded as he watched the angry flush on his agents' face.

"Captain Ruiz was right, your so damn good at your job that no one or anything frightens you and everyone can go to hell as far as your concern. All right Agent Cruse, I called you in because the Americans have a major problem and they leaned on us hard. I have been in this position for eleven years and this is the first time I have ever received a call from our President personally."

Chapter 5

Alex looked down at the papers he held half crushed in his hand. Chuck Witt had looked so smug when the lawyer handed me the papers. He had tried to look concerned but now I can see it was just the opposite, he was gloating. Why? Where did that come from, twenty some years we worked together building this company. He was going to be rich, why would he also want my half?

Alex went over the conversation that had taken place less than half an hour ago that turned his world upside down. He had been looking forward to the meeting with Chuck and the lawyers, they had finally decided it was time to take the money and run. Well, not run really, they would still own 20% of the company, 10% for each partner and they wanted to keep their fingers on the pulse of the company by being allowed to have an office in the company and a title of Senior Consultants.

But the other 40% that each was going to get was close to fifty-five million apiece. But not anymore if Chuck got his way as Alex picked up the conversation in his mind.

"Alex, there's just no other way to say it so I'll just spit it out. For the last five years I've been buying up the options we both signed with each other years ago. Those options give me control of the company and our agreement on the option's state that if one partner exercises these options the other partner has two choices. One, he can go along with the first partner and be paid two times the last fiscal year's net profit for his share in the company. The second choice would be to purchase all the outstanding notes still owed by the company from 1st National Bank and then the shoe would be on the other foot." Alex sat looking at Chuck for a long time trying to figure out just what it was he was saying. Here he thought they were in the final phase of selling the company for millions of dollars and Chuck was telling him he now owned the company and was kicking him out!

"What are you saying Chuck? I'm not going to go along with that. Our net profit was less than half a million dollars. You know that, we've plowed every penny back into the company, that would mean you would only have to come up with a million dollars and the whole company would be yours."

"Than you have the second choice Alex, buy up all the notes held by 1st National Bank."

"Buy up all the notes from 1st National! God damn it Chuck, we just renewed the notes to 1st National three months ago and on your insistence we took out a 10 million-dollar loan to purchase all the new assembly line equipment. That's thirty million dollars in notes, how could I come up with the cash to pay off the notes unless I mortgaged the company. And I can't do that because you hold the options."

"I'm sorry Alex but I had to look after myself and my family, the last five years you have been taking on more and more of the responsibility and running of the company. You only call me in when you have to have me sign something. I felt you were trying to push me out."

"Push you out! Chuck, you're the one that kept complaining about too much work and you never had time for your family or to play golf. I never told you to not come in, it was always you calling in and telling me you needed time off. Sure I complained to you about it, I felt like I was doing most of the work, but I never pushed you out or told you not to come to work. Come on Chuck wake up and stop this stupid business before we both get hurt."

"Oh I'm stopping it all right Alex. Tom give Alex the copies of the agreement and the letters he signed. You remember Tom Brush, don't you Alex. He's my family lawyer and he's been helping me for the last five years." Tom Brush leaned over and handed Alex copies of the agreement he and Chuck had signed years ago,

Alex looked dumbstruck and did not reach out for the documents.

"Mr. Bell, I'm sure you remember but just in case you forgot, I will remind you, you have ninety days to exercise one of the two choices. If you fail to do either than Mr. Witt will have the option of giving you a certified check for the amount of ownership in the company, which will be approximately one million dollars." Alex watch as the lawyer put the papers down in front of him. He watched as the lawyer and Witt turned and left the room. Stunned he sat there for a full five minutes letting it soak in what his partner had done to him. He had set him up over a long period of time and now the pay off was coming. That's when he felt the bile starting to rise and his heart began to race and he found it hard to breath. Grabbing the papers he lounged from the chair and fled down the outside stairs. Sitting on the bench he looked again at the papers and wondered what he was going to tell him wife and kids.

Chapter 6

Shelby wiped the sweat from her face before raising the binocular to her eyes and studying the two men strolling close to the large doors going into the big house. Each carried the M16 used by the United States Military. It was a highly accurate gun and capable of emptying it's load in less than ten seconds. Shelby never gave the guns or men a second thought for she knew her skills were far beyond anything that they were capable of doing. They would be dead before a shot would be fired or a shout could be heard from either man, and she could do it from far or up close. In a few minutes the phone call would be coming and maybe they would get what they sent her out there to hear.

Shelby scanned the larger man as he walked in her direction some eight hundred yards away, as the crow fly's, for she was on one hill and he was on the other with the small village below and between them both.

She adjusted the power to get a close up of his face just to make sure she did not see a large white scar running from his eye to his jaw. No scar was found, but when the other man said something the man she was watching smiled, a smile that sent bolts of anger through her body. The smile was the same as the smile of the man who had killed the monkey when she was young; She had learned that all the cruel ones had that same smile.

Another memory flooded forth from deep in the recesses of her brain as she saw that same smile on the scar face man holding her daddy by his elbows as he stood before Hector King in the small clearing before the hut they lived in. Her daddy was shaking his head and kept repeating that he had told no one. But Hector King would not let up as he repeated the same phrase over and over. "Who else have you told about the shipment." Each time he asked the question and her daddy gave the same answer the man with the ugly smile and scar would bend his elbows further behind him until he screamed. Shelby was hidden behind a large palm tree that had fallen the day before, some twenty-five feet away and watched as the big man hurt her daddy over and over. After what seemed like hours she watched as they picked her daddy up and half carried, half dragged him up the road to the big house and through the big doors. She never saw her daddy again she was six years old at the time.

Shelby had loved her daddy so much; he would always bring her something sweet from the big cities every time he took a trip. He would always leave with a large sack strapped to his back and a big smile to his little girl as he walked away into the jungle and the two to three week trip to his destination. Her daddy had even been to the United States before she was born. That is how she ended up with the unusual first name she had. Her daddy had fallen in love with the powerful Mustang sport car he was allowed to use while in the United States in a city called Houston. He had returned with large posters of the Mustang and when Shelby was born her small corner of the shack was decorated with these pictures. The name Shelby had come from the man responsible for one type of the powerful muscle car.

Shelby took a deep sigh as the memories flooded back of the pretty white dress her mother held up for her to put on when she was nine. Shelby was thrilled to see what her mother had for her to wear but the emotions were mixed for she also saw the tears in her mother's eyes and the sadness etched on her face. Flashes of memories raced through her brain, memories of horror, of bright red stains on her pretty dress and thighs. Memories of running as fast as she could down the road from the big house to her mother's house and the additional horror that waited her there. Shelby shook her head from side to side slinging sweat in both directions as if she could throw the ugly memories from her head.

Chapter 7

"As I said Agent Cruse, this is the first time I have received a call from the President. His instructions to me was very straightforward, I am to assign the best agent in the country too this job. We are to give the Americans every bit of information we have now and will get in the future on this case. You are the best agent we have and I told the President I would have you on the job by tomorrow."

"An that job would be what Director?"

"The job is to find this drug dealer, find out when the next shipment is coming and terminate both."

"Terminate both! To make it clear Director, you mean I am to find out when and where the next shipment is coming from this dealer and destroy it. In addition, I am to kill the dealer. Where is this dealer? In our country or somewhere else."

"The dealer is in our country."

"In our country! I believe there is a law in our country that states very clearly that we are not to assassinate our own citizens Director. Would you care to explain that to me sir."

"Agent Cruse there are times when you have to go above the law for the good of your country. An by the good of our country I mean the United States has strongly suggested that this man does not live beyond tomorrow or the next day. Is that clear enough for you Agent Cruse?"

"So, the big bully United States calls our President and tells him, no demands that he kill one of his own citizens because of the half-ass job they have done. Sorry Director but I will have nothing to do with assassinations. I might be ruthless, as you say, and kill anyone who attacked me while doing my job, but I have never put a gun to a mans head and killed him without first seeing if the man wanted to surrender."

"Do you have any idea what the United States could do to our country if we refused. With the flick of their finger they could make our economy go down the tub by pulling our aid package just for this year alone."

"I don't care what the United States could do to us, I will not become your hired assassin!"

"Agent Cruse you will obey these orders, I'm not Captain Ruiz, I am the Director and if you do not obey this command you will find yourself answering phone calls in a one woman office in the remotest office we have. By God who do you think you are anyway, this country has given you the best education in the world and granted every request you ever ask for."

"I am well aware what my country has done for me Director and I would lay down my life if it called for that in any job assigned to me. Why would you let the United States bring us to that level, no matter what the cost? Who is this drug dealer that he can command such a moral price from our country?"

"The man ordered two of their agents to be killed to protect his drugs, Agent Cruse, that alone should be enough for him to be targeted for death. Another reason I assigned this job to you is because he lives in your old stomping grounds. Or at lease close to where the family that adopted you found you and because you have had extensive experience in the jungle. The name he goes by, or at lease that we know him by is Hector King and he lives somewhere close to the city of Mitu."

Director Gozares noticed the pupil's of her eyes expanding until they held almost fifty percent of her total eyes. Then the color drained from her face as her body stiffened and her eyes bore into his. *Wow! He thought, what nerve did I hit, but before he could say anything she spoke.*

"Who will be my contact." That's all she said as the Director continued to look at her.

"Would you care to explain your sudden change of heart Agent Cruse?"

"No!"

"No! You practically tell me to go to hell when I gave you an order and then when I tell you where and who the assignment is you make a 180 degree turn and ask only who your contact will be?"

"What the hell is going on here Agent Cruse? Why is this place so important because---damn, it's not the place is it? It's the name Hector King. Who is Hector King Agent Cruse?"

"I don't know who Hector King is Director, I've only heard his name in rumors when people talk about big drug pushers." *She's lying through her teeth*, the Director thinks as he watches her for any other signs before remembering something in her file.

Director Gozares opened her file again and begins to scan until he comes to the information he vaguely remembers from his first reading of her file. "It mentions that you told your adoptive family a few months after you were found that you lived in the jungle for close to eighteen months all by yourself. No adults to help you find food or shelter or to help you survive, how is it a nine and ten year old could survive for eighteen months in the jungle alone? Did this Hector King help? Was he living in the jungle at the same time you were?"

"No! I, I lived alone, no one was with me."

"You're a liar Agent Cruse, no nine and ten year old girl could have survived in the jungle alone and no nine or ten year old child could have known how to make the bow and arrows and the rock knife you had when your adoptive family found you." Shelby never took her eyes from his nor did she blink, she also said nothing. He noticed she never blinked and that unnerved him for some reason.

"I told you at the beginning of our meeting something did not smell right with you and your file Agent Cruse, you know this man, I know you do. Is he your father?" That made Shelby give a horselaugh as she continued to stare at the Director without blinking and her body positioned, not changed from the moment she hear the name of Hector King, posed like a snake ready to strike.

Never in his thirty-seven years as an agent, many on dangerous undercover assignments, had he felt the certainly that he felt at this moment, the certainly that if she decided to attack he would be dead almost before his brain realized she was moving towards him. It was a very odd feeling, one of slight fear but also one of admiration for a fellow agent that had the capability to evoke those feelings. Without any further hesitation his mind was made up and he was satisfied not to go any deeper into what he knew must be a very deep dark hole in her mind.

"Your contact man will be Captain Ruiz, because you work well together and you know each others quirks he is the logical choice. He is waiting down stairs to take you to the plane, you will have to parachute into the jungle some ten miles north of the last transmission the Americans have given us for his location. You will have the equipment to patch directly into the Americans communications; any thing you record will also be transmitted not only to Captain Ruiz and me but also to the head of the team working on it from their end. Any questions?"

"No Sir."

"Good luck Agent Cruse, and there's no confusion or conflict about both jobs you are to complete?"

"No Sir!"

The Director only nodded as he pressed a button and the door opened telling her it was time to leave.

Chapter 8

Vera stood by the window watching her husband, Alex, drop his keys twice before he finally inserted one into the car door and turned the key to lock it. She continued to watch as he stumbled up the walk to their house. For some reason she couldn't understand Alex had parked the car half way up the circular drive way instead of driving to the side of the house where the circular drive split off to the five car garage in the back. Vera knew something was wrong for a couple of reasons. One was that it was now eleven-thirty on a Wednesday night and second he was drunk. Although she was use to him working long hours he was almost always home before nine and he never went out drinking with people from work. Even when they would go out for the night Alex never drink more than one glass of wine or one shot of whiskey or it's equivalent.

If he drank at home it was the same, one drink that was the limit he had always placed on himself. He had always told her he never liked the feeling he got if he had more than one and so for the last twenty-five years that had been his limit. With a little fear and a little anger in her heart Vera waited and listened as he tried to insert the front door key in the lock. After a few attempts she walked from the front window to the door and yanked it opened as Alex was mumbling to himself. Vera had to catch him because he had been leaning against the door as he tried to put another key into the slot.

After a few sloppy attempts to kiss her and tell her how pretty she looked Vera guided him to the front room couch and let him slip from her arms to the soft cushions where he immediately slid off to the floor. There she let him sit while she took the chair facing him and waited. After getting no response from him for more than five minutes Vera went to the kitchen and made a pot of instance coffee that she poured half in and half on him. When he started to protest in earnest she sat back down in the chair and waited for him to start talking. Instead he began to cry and tell her how sorry he was.

When Vera finally got the full story from him she just held him and told him they still had each other and things would work out. If they had to they could sell this big house and move back to the kind of houses they had been living in for the first fifteen years of their marriage. They would be as happy, just as long as they had each other.

The next morning Alex and Vera were talking and going over the different scenarios on the company and what his partner, Chuck Witt, had done to them. "Vera, your close to Sara, would you go and talk to her and try to get her to make Chuck see what he is doing is wrong."

"I don't think it will do any good Alex. I think she knew what was happening, last week I called her to see where she wanted to meet for our regular weekly lunch and she hemmed and laughed around and finally said she had something else she needed to do. I really never thought anything about it until just now. Now I know why she was avoiding me, she knew what Chuck was planning to do to us. Are you sure there's nothing we can do to stop him Alex, I will look over the documents but you should call our family attorney?

"Oh, I plan to do just that today Vera, but deep down I don't think he will find anything we can do. Chuck knew what he was doing and for God sakes he had five years to get all the things written exactly how he and his attorney wanted. No, I don't think there's anything we can do, I just don't understand why someone would want to do what he did just to get a large sum of money when he was going to have a great deal coming to him in a few months anyway."

"Of course you can't understand it Alex, your not a thief, you don't have a mean bone in your body. And don't you dare say you should have seen it coming, no one would have seen something like that. We don't look on our friends as thieves or someone who wants to hurt you. What kind of world would we live in if we believed that, always looking over our shoulder to see who was doing what to us or our family. If we have to Alex we'll take the million and start a small business that we both can work in, we'll make a decent living and we will be happy."

"We've always been able to work things out together Vera, and your right, we'll make it in spite of what Chuck is trying to do to us. Thanks for standing beside me and understanding, a lot of wives would have been screaming their heads off about the life they would have to give up."

That afternoon Alex stood and shook hands with an attorney and friend of many years and thanked him for spending the time to look over the papers he had dropped off earlier in the day. The news was as Alex had expected; he had signed away his company unless he could come up with close to thirty million dollars to buy the notes at the bank. And he knew that was impossible, for without using the company as collateral he had no chance. Chuck had made sure that possibility was also zero for Alex.

Alex needed to run to blow off steam and relax, running was his way of relaxing but the weather had turned bad and was raining hard, as it did a lot in April in Oklahoma City. Alex watched the weather report at ten o'clock and saw the rain was to stop sometime around midnight. He pushed down on the alarm button, more out of habit than anything, which would go off at four-thirty in the morning. That was when he liked to run, no people, no cars, and just the first few notes of the early birds beginning to sing.

By four-forty-five A.M. Alex was out the door and starting his regular six-mile run through the neighborhood. He loved the sounds and smells accompanying him on his run. One mile into his run he knew that the lady that lived in the small brick home on the corner was already up and dressed because he could smell the heavy perfume she put on every morning. It was funny, he had never met the woman but he knew some of her habits down to the minute. If he was five minutes late leaving his house for his run her light in the bathroom would be out and the one in the kitchen would be on and he could smell bacon frying. If he was on time the bathroom light would be on and he would smell perfume only. When he made his loop and returned past her house at the five mile mark he could see the steam coming from her washer, because she always turned it on right after turning on her front room lights. That was a ritual she had completed for a number of years, at lease in the years Alex had ran this route.

The air was heavy because of the rain the evening before and this caused the smells and the sounds to magnify in his senses. Alex was a million miles away in thoughts as he turned the corner and almost ran into the back of a large moving van parked half in the road and half on the grass. The truck was parked at an angle with the back wheels just off the sidewalk and the front ones over the sidewalk, partially covering the grass. Alex had to push his hand out to redirect his running towards the front of the truck. He had less than two feet between the front fender and the wire fence surrounding the yard it was parked by. As he slowed to squeeze through the small gap he turned his head and got a quick glimpse of a man standing by the driver's door, leaning into the cab, with a stricken look on his face.

You ought to look shocked you dumb bastard, Alex thought as he finally squeezed through the small opening before increasing his speed back to normal. *You shouldn't be driving such a big truck if you don't know how to handle a turn, your just lucky no one's awake in the house to see the tracks you put on the lawn,* Alex mumbled to himself.

For the next two miles Alex relaxed and let his mind go to his body as he mentally checked his strides, breathing, pace, rhythm and balance. When he got in this state it was as if he was outside his body watching the well oiled runner running with the efficiently of someone who has ran fast and hard for many years. His pulse and heart rate hardly rose as he turned at the end of his designated three miles and began his journey back.

The Oklahoma City Memorial Marathon was one week away and Alex's hard training was over, this morning and the next four mornings would be a fast but relaxed six miles. No more eighteen and twenty mile runs and no hills to struggle up or hills to go down and feeling the muscles in the back of your legs protest that down hill running was not as fun as it looked. Alex had run each of the six Memorial Marathons, dedicating each run to a different friend who had died in the Federal Building when the deranged but very competent Timothy McVeigh exploded a bomb under the second floor day care center. Snuffing out the lives of the small innocent children playing their first games of the new day. Eleven of Alex's friends died that morning, leaving behind twenty-four children and ten wives to mourn and ask questions that will never be answered.

Coming back down the street where the truck had stopped Alex turned from the sidewalk and ran down the middle of the street. The truck was still in the same position as when he had first saw it but as he got closer he could not see that anyone was standing by the door nor could he see anyone in the truck. The lights were still on and Alex could hear the motor still running. As Alex ran past the open door he took a quick glance and saw that the man was now lying inside the truck with his legs sticking completely out from the seat. It even looked, they way the body was twisted, that the man's head might be hanging down from the seat towards the floorboard on the passengers side.

Alex maintained his speed as he passed the truck and turned the corner for the last mile to his house. *Maybe Alex thought there was something wrong with the guy.* He remembered the stricken look on his face when he pasted the first time and thought it was because he never made the turn and almost ran through a fence. But now Alex wasn't so sure, maybe the stricken look was because he was sick.

Alex ran for another half-mile before deciding the man might be really sick and would need help. Alex turned and ran back to the corner where the truck was. Once he came to the corner he slowed to a walk and slowly came up to the driver's side. The man was still there and he was not moving, Alex could now see he was indeed lying with his head almost touching the floorboard on the passenger's side.

"Hello, do you need some help." Alex said, but he received no answer from the man. Alex grabbed the hand latch and pulled himself up on the running board to get a better look. Again he spoke to the man.

"Hello, do you need any help." This time Alex received a reply, a soft moan as the man tried to raise his head. Alex reached down and grabbed the man's shoulders and slowly pulled him to a sitting position. The man tried to say something but no words came out as Alex noticed the yellow spittle dripping from the corner of his mouth. Finally the man opened his eyes and looked at Alex with blood shot eyes.

"Help me please, med—med---"he tried to say before finally getting the words out.

"Medicine, Nitroglycerin, in the glove compartment, I'm having a heart att-attack, please help me."

Alex put one arm under the man's legs and the other behind his back and lifted him until he was resting against the passenger's door. Then he jabbed the button to the glove compartment and reached in, searching for a bottle almost before the door opened. Feeling through the stack of papers in the compartment he felt from right to left and was about to say to the man that there was no bottle in there when in the very corner his fingers felt the round top of a medicine bottle.

The man's skin was turning blue by the time Alex opened the bottle and placed one pill under the man's tongue. He found a bottle of water lying on the dash up against the window, apparently where the man had dropped it when he was trying to get it opened before he passed out. The bottle cap was off and only a few mouthfuls of water were left but that was enough. As soon as Alex felt the pill had dissolved in his mouth he gave him the bottle and watched as he drank the last few drops.

Alex could see his color was already becoming normal but he was so weak he could hardly raise his arms. Alex looked around and finally spotted what he was looking for. The man had a cell phone jacket but no phone was there. Looking some more Alex spied the phone lying on the floor by the gas pedal and picked it up to dial nine one one when the man grabbed his hand.

"No, please don't call the ambulance, I'm getting better by the minute, the pill is working good. I just need a place to rest for a few hours. Do you live around here?"

"Yes, I live just down the street about a mile from here, but we need to get you to a doctor or a hospital mister." Alex again tried to dial nine one one when the man folded his hand over the phone and Alex's hand. With his other hand the man reached inside a paper bag lying inside the large cup holder in front of the dash, a bag that Alex had not noticed before.

"Please, just drive me to your home so I can rest for a few hours." Then he pulled his hand from the bag and put something over the phone Alex was holding. "Please take this, it's all yours if you will help me to your house and let me rest for a few hours, then I will be on my way."

Alex looked down at the object the man had placed in his hand. Alex's first reaction was, *you're giving me Monopoly money?* But when he looked closer he knew it was not Monopoly money, it was a small bundle of one hundred dollar bills wrapped with a small band like the bands banks put on stacks of bills before sending them out. And the band was marked with the amount in the stack. The number read ten thousand dollars.

"Take it please, it's all yours, let me rest for a few hours, than I'm gone, I promise you."

Alex tried to protest again but the man insisted so Alex, shaking his head, moved to the drivers seat and closed the big truck door. Five minutes later he was driving up his driveway to the side of his house where he parked the truck. All the way home he darted glances at the man but he had not moved. His head and body was resting against the door and his eyes were closed. Alex noticed that Vera had already left, she had told him she was going to see her mother who lived in Kingfisher. A town about forty miles away and would stay for the three days her mother would be in the hospital for a small female surgery she had been putting off far to long. Vera had finally made the appointment for her and told her she would be there to take her and say until she was back home and rested for a day or two.

Alex turned to the sleeping man and was trying to decide whether to let him sleep where he was or wake him up and help him to a bed. He decided the man needed to be in a bed so Alex reached over and shook the man.

"Mister, were at my house, I'll come around to the passenger's side and help you down, Ok?" Alex did not get a response and when he looked closer he noted his color was again turning blue. Quickly reaching over Alex put his finger on his neck and felt for a pulse. None was found. He bent his head to the man's chest and listened for a heart beat. None was found. Almost in a panic Alex beat on the man's chest four times but no reaction came from the man. Alex laid the man on his back across the seat, whipped the spittle from the corner of his mouth and started mouth-to-mouth. Alex tried for ten minutes but to no avail. When he raised his head and looked down at the man he knew he was dead and nothing was going to bring him back. Already his skin was beginning to feel cold and clammy.

Alex sat for minutes staring at the man and wondering why this had happened to him, didn't he have enough trouble with what happened yesterday with his partner, Chuck Witt. Now he had a dead man and his truck in his driveway and even scarier he had ten thousand dollars in one hundred dollar bills in his pocket. Alex began going through his pockets but he found nothing out of the ordinary. The last pocket he searched he found the man's billfold with a number of papers inside along with a California's driver's license. When he checked under the drivers seat he got a small surprise, wrapped in cloth was a small snub nose 32 caliber pistol with five live rounds and one spent cartridge. Alex wrapped the gun with the cloth before dumping it in one of his garbage sacks that he than placed in the trash bend. No way anyone would find that gun after it was taken to the landfill the next trash pickup day.

Sitting in the truck with the billfold in his hand he glanced down at the paper sack that a few minutes ago produced a stack of one hundred bills worth ten thousands dollars. Opening the sack Alex's pulse quickened as he saw four more stacks and each one had the same kind of band and the same figure written on each. *My God* he though, there's another forty thousand dollars in the sack. What was this guy into? Where was he going in a moving van? What was he carrying in the van?

Alex started the truck up and pulled it around the garage to a large shed that he had built for the motor home they were about to buy, that is before yesterday happened, he had to get the truck out of sight, the neighborhood would be waking up soon. When Alex had the truck inside he stepped out of the truck and went to the back. There he found a lock had been placed on the two large swinging doors. Looking around to find something he could smash or cut the lock off he found the crowbar he had used the month before to pry open a sealed metal barrel. As he was putting the crowbar between the lock and the door he stopped. Dropping the crowbar he went back to the cab and searched it to see if there was a key that would open the door. Alex found no such key and was walking back to the end of the truck when he reached inside his pocket and pulled out the truck keys. Dangling from the ring was a different kind of key it definitely was not a truck key Alex thought. Alex inserted the key into the lock and turned. With a relief smile he felt the lock turn and watched as the lock sprung open.

Chapter 9

Director Gozares watched the feed coming in from the helicopter pad as Agent Cruse and Captain Ruiz stepped into the passenger's seats and fastens their belts. As they began to lift off he raised the phone and made the call to the president's office. He had done what he was told to do and now it was up to the best agent he had to carry out the orders. Director Gozares was still seizing with rage from the orders he had received from the vice-president two days ago. Never in his years in law enforcement had he been ordered to assassinate another human. Kill if they could not be captured or killed in a firefight was the way the game was played, but to deliberately send out an agent to assassinate someone with no other option was illegal and wrong. It could lead you down a slippery road that could drag the country into chaos. He had witnessed such chaos as a young agent working in Chile in the late seventies.

Thousands of men, woman and even children simply disappeared and were never heard from again. And the repercussions were still being felt today in that country.

For a while in his office, sitting across from Agent Cruse, he had hope that she would not obey his order and at first that's just what she did. Then something happened and her mind was changed one hundred percent. Something so strong happened in her that it changed her whole world, something from her past that was not in the report he had before him.

Director Gozares punched the gold button under his desk and relaxed back into his chair. From the central wall in front of his desk a screen came down and the film started. The camera was mounted directly behind and above the Directors desk and was focused on the middle chair in front of him. He studied the film three times, watching very intently the moment he mentioned the name of Hector King. An absolute change, something exploded in Agent Cruse's mind at that moment. This had to do with her childhood; there is nothing in her file from the time she was found by the Bazzaren family until today that would have caused such a change.

What could have happened to a young girl that would make such a change! Many things, the Director thought, but most likely she was raped and from her reaction, very violently. This Hector King was a large drug dealer but he was far from the big cities and kept himself and his operation from the law's eyes. Of course, in the area he operated from he was the law, but still, there was no record of any kind of arrest of him or his mules. He was just one of many large drug dealers in his country and his operations help the economy. The Director shook his head, if only the smart people would get smart, especially the one's in the United States. They were pouring billions of dollars into our country to stop the drug trade and billions in military aid and equipment and yet nothing stopped the flow. And nothing would ever stop the flow of drugs from his country into the United States. Someday they would all wake up and understand that a poor farmer making one hundred and fifty dollars a year on his farm could plant one acre of cocoa plant and sell the crop for ten times what he would make on anything else he planted. The buyer would then mix the plant with other ingredients to make Heroin, which he would then sell to a dealer for another ten times what he paid the farm. The Dealer in turn would distribute the Heroin by men, called mules, to the far shores of the United States. When you could make more in one month than you could in a lifetime doing anything else, what did the smart people think would happen? You want to stop the trafficking in drugs across the world, very simple, make it legal and tax it.

The Director shook his head as he thought about that, the smart people, why can't they see that. A perfect example was what the United States did in the late

1920's; they passed a law prohibiting the consumption of alcohol across America. Alcohol was cheap before that and anyone that wanted a bottle could buy one. After the law was passed everything went underground and the prices soared. But the important thing was the people and the violence that came from it. The United States are still dealing with the gangs that came from that area, they called them the families and the killings that came from it was terrific. When the United States reversed the prohibition law's the killing's stopped and the prices came back down. The only problem they had after that was that the families just branched off into other illegal adventures and then they found the best friend they ever had drugs.

The smart people, they read the newspapers every day and learn about the killings and robberies through out the world that's connected to the drug trade. But there not smart enough to see that they are not reading about killings and robberies from alcohol, and that's because alcohol is legal and taxed. A person does not have to kill to get their supply of alcohol, nor can they buy a truckload and sell it to the public for a fantastic profit.

Director Gozares turned his attention back to the film and studied it over for the fourth time before shutting it off. She's the best agent I have and in a few days I will have her report on my desk stating the mission was competed, he was sure.

Captain Ruiz went over the last of the equipment Shelby would be carrying on this mission when the red light came on. The helicopter was hovering over the drop zone some ten miles from where the signals were coming from. He gave her thumbs up as she attached the rope to her harness and slipped over the side. Shelby was dangling two hundred feet from the floor of the jungle but only twenty some feet above the trees. She had to be very careful as she lowered herself between two massive trees with branches that tried to reach out and snag her or her equipment.

Once on the ground she disconnected the rope and gave a salute to Captain Ruiz as the helicopter begin to rise and fall away from her eyesight. In less than a minute she could no longer hear the motor. After checking her equipment she looked at the compass attached to her right wrist and headed in the direction the signals had come from. The compass was really not necessary; she could navigate in the jungle almost blindfolded. As she walked her mind and her body begin to emerge with her surroundings and she became a silent stalker moving through the jungle. Only someone raised in the jungle could flow with the branches and trees and not be heard. Shelby could walk less than five feet past another person in this environment and they would neither hear nor see her. The old skills came back the minute she stepped on the jungle floor and her body reacted in the same way. This was good, this was safe territory to be in when you are alone and her senses were fully alert. Following trails that no one else could see, trails made by animals,

Shelby moved fast and silently for the first six miles. Then she came upon a fast flowing creek ten to fifteen feet wide and five to seven feet deep. To swift and deep to try and swim it with the equipment she carried, Shelby scanned the area and decided to go up stream to find the crossing she needed. Thirty minutes later she found what she was looking for, a large tree had fallen, half in and half out of the water, but more important, there were trees on the opposite bank.

Standing as far out on the falling tree as she could she pulled a small rope from her pack and made a large loop from one end, raising it over her head. Making a circling motion three times until the rope was whistling in the air, than with a twist of her wrist she flung the looped end towards the top of the smallest tree and watched as it hit its mark and began to slide down the trunk. With a strong jerk Shelby tightened the rope around the tree and then tested the rope by pulling hard a number of times. When the rope stayed in place she backed to the end of the fallen tree before shooting forward as fast as she could on the tree. Pulling her legs under her she went with the momentum that flung her past the tree on the other side and to solid ground on the other bank. Smiling she remembered doing that a number of times trying to escape the pack of boys that were always in the mood to hurt her.

Shelby reached her destination at two-thirty in the morning. Standing on the hill overlooking the small valley below she could, by the light of the full moon, just make out a few scattered huts and of course she could see the large house on the opposite hill from where she stood. She unpacked and separated her gear before bedding down in a make shift bed made of palm leaves. She slept like a baby among the night sounds that had been so familiar to her so long ago.

Chapter 10

For a few seconds Alex stood looking at the open lock on the big swinging doors of the truck, *what the hell was he doing*? He had a dead man in the front of the truck and now he was breaking into someone else's property. As much as it bothered him he knew he was going to open those doors and find out what a man who carried fifty thousands dollars in his cab would be carry in the back. Lifting the lock from the slot he swung the big doors open and looked inside. The truck was packed to the roof with boxes two feet wide and three feet deep and he was sure the boxes went clear to the front. There were no markings on any of the boxes in the front rows, just clear plastic tape covering the lids. Alex went to the front of the building and picked up a small ladder, on his way back he grabbed a carpet knife and a crowbar before putting them all down on the floor behind the truck. As he adjusted the ladder he stopped, turned and walked back to the front passenger door and looked in at the man lying dead. Alex opened the door and carefully felt around his neck for any pulse, Alex never expected to feel one but he was beginning to get paranoid with every thing that had happened. Satisfied that the man was really dead Alex turned and went back to the back of the truck and climbed three steps of the ladder to where he could then hook the crowbar between the top box and the one beside it. By pulling slowly and descending the ladder he was able to pull the top box down without moving the one beside it. With a soft thud the box hit the floor of the building and rolled on its side for a few feet before stopping upright.

Alex walked around the box four times looking at it and wondering what was inside. At lease he knew it wasn't something breakable or if it was the packaging was good. His heart began to race as he took the carpet knife and sliced through the clear plastic tape down the middle. Then he inserted the knife under the edge and cut the tape holding the flaps on both sides. Alex thought he knew what was in the boxes, no one drove around in a big truck, and an out of state one at that, with fifty thousand in cash on his person. This man was carrying drugs from one state to another and he was sure the boxes were full of both marijuana and hard drugs. What he would do with them he had no idea, for he had never been associated with anyone who even sold marijuana. A few of his friends still smoke marijuana but neither he nor Vera had touched one after college.

His mind was racing with the thought, what if this is all marijuana and other drugs, could I find someone to buy the load? How much would this be worth? Would I have the guts to even try? They put you in prison and they throw away the keys when you try to sell a large quantity of drugs. No he couldn't jeopardize his reputation, or hurt his family in that way, no way he was going to try and sell it. So hot shot, what do you do now, you just walk up to the police and tell them what happened, that's what you do. Even the fifty thousand dollars you turn over, that should be enough to convince them you have nothing to do with him or the truck.

Feeling good with his decision Alex flipped back the two flaps and every muscle in his body froze. He finally got his eyes to blink only because he thought if he blinked and looked again it would go away or he would see something else. Didn't happen, it was still there. Alex blinked a few more times before he reached down and laid his hands on the objects, then he began to shake all over until he had to sit down on the hard concrete floor.

When Alex felt he had control of his body he leaned over and put his face close to the objects in the box and starred at it for a long time. Now the adrenaline begun to course through his body as his mind began to race with what he had and what it could me for him, his family and the company.

Alex began lifting the objects from the box until he had them all neatly stacked just like they had been in the box and then he began to count. Twenty objects high, ten objects wide and five objects long, all with neat ten thousand dollar bands around them. Alex looked around to find something to write with when he spied a small white rock on the floor a few feet away. Grabbing the rock he started his calculations. Twenty times ten times five times ten thousand came to----he was stunned when he saw the figure.

Sitting on the floor Alex rolled the number over in his head a number of times to get a grip on what it was he had, he took the small piece of rock and did the calculations a second time. He got the same results; the amount sitting before him was exactly one hundred million dollars. One hundred million! Alex turned his head and looked at the large number of boxes in the truck and he tried to guess the amount but gave up because his brain was not working very well at the moment.

Seven hours later Alex had dragged the last of the boxes from the moving van and added the count to the others. There were one hundred and eighty-three boxes in all. Most of the value was in the first eight boxes he opened for in those were the one hundred-dollar bills, the rest included all the other denominations from the one dollar bill to the fifty. In all Alex counted two billion, one hundred and seventeen million dollars. Every packet neatly rapped with the denomination and total. That was the only way Alex finished in seven hours, if he had to count each bill he would have been at it when his wife came home in a few days.

In the seven hours he was pulling boxes and counting money he went from being giddy to afraid to paranoid and finally to numb. After taking a shower and eating a light lunch Alex tried to take a nap but found it was useless to try. His mind would not stop spinning and he finally went back to the building and walked among the money. He knew he had to do something with the truck and the dead body, but what was the best thing to do to make sure nothing came back to him. By now Alex knew he was not going to the police, all that money changed his mind very quickly. He knew it was drug money and he also knew people were looking for it. He decided he would wait until dark and then drive the truck to some mall and park it. But first he had to dump the body somewhere, would it be better to leave the body in the truck? Or would it be better to leave it somewhere far away from the truck so the police would not connect the truck with the dead man.

Alex put the money back in the boxes and stacked the boxes against one wall of the building before opening the doors to the building. He had decided it would be better to go just after dark, that way it would still be evening and people would be out shopping and not notice a large moving van going by them or being parked. If he waited until two or three in the morning he would be taking the chance of someone remembering a large truck out at that time of the night. In addition, the police would be more alert if a vehicle came by at that time of night.

Sitting on one of the boxes of money Alex felt ashamed to know he was the kind of person who would steal. All his life he had been honest, not once had he ever taken something that did not belong to him and yet sitting on a box of money he could see he was justifying his actions. The money belong to someone who got it illegal and that person never deserved it anymore than he did. What should he do, take it to the police, they would end up spending it like all governments did. Most would be wasted; well he knew it wouldn't be wasted if he kept it.

That was another problem he was going to have, how could he spend it, the government kept track of any transactions above nine thousand nine hundred and ninety-nine dollars. How could he take this money to the bank to pay off the notes without explaining how he got the cash. He couldn't show any withdraws in that amount and they would only believe so much of it might be winnings at the casinos. No, he couldn't do it that way; he had to find some way to hide the money, but how and where?

Chapter 11

The call came right on time, Shelby picked up the signal before the big house on the hill answered the phone and her recording was going. Every thing she heard was also being heard by Director Gozares and the American team somewhere in Houston.

"Hello."

"Mr. King please."

"Hold."

"This is King Speaking."

"Jose Manual, Mr. King.

"Hello Jose, I was expecting your call two days ago, when did Doug Ringo and Hernando Kling delivered the merchandise?"

"There's a problem Mr. King."

"What kind of problem Jose."

"The merchandise has not been delivered and we have not seen Doug Ringo or Hernando Kling."

"Which part of the merchandise is missing Jose? Are you in contact with any of the five merchants?"

"I have contacted all five merchants Mr. King. Each delivered their merchandise to the one control; the last was more than two days ago. All verified the signatures were authentic, the correct control picked up all five shipments and all were transferred to their possession."

"And you have heard nothing from the control?"

"No Sir, not a peep. The last report from the final merchant was that they were heading towards Houston as planned. I have linked into the highway patrol in Texas but so far no hit's on our vehicle."

"You have twenty-four hours to find them Mr. Manual, you understand me, twenty-four hours to find them and our merchandise."

"Let me remind you Mr. King you were the one that insisted that two of your men would be the final control. I do not take kindly to threats Mr. King; I'm as deeply committed to this as you are. Don't forget I to have merchandise that is missing. We are doing every thing we can do at this end; we will find both men and the merchandise that I promise you. But I need to point out to you Mr. King; I was against moving five different groups of merchandise into one control. It was entirely against my wishes."

"I counted on you to see the job was done right Mr. Manual, you have failed me. Do I have to come there to see the job finished?"

"You are welcome to come Mr. King but you will only be in the way, you do not know the territory or the people. Please, stay where you are and I will keep you informed about the merchandise."

"We have been in business for a long time my friend, I hope the kind of merchandise being delivered did not turn you from that friendship. I will wait for your call."

As the line went dead Shelby pushed the transmission that would send the voices to both Director Gozares and the American team. She had no doubt they both all ready had the recording but that was her job, any calls coming in or out were to be recorded and transmitted to the two locations. But the one piece of information she needed confirmed was confirmed. The target was in the house on the hill and she would make her way there as soon as darkness came.

Squatting with her field glasses in her hand Shelby spent the afternoon scanning back and forth the area from the road leading from the village to the hill top house. She knew where every guard was and what time they would be changing. When she was satisfied she knew all she needed to know about the house she then reluctantly turned her glasses to the small village and the tiny shack now occupied by others where memories of so much terror filled her mind.

Scanning the ground around the shack she had lived in for almost nine years she spotted the small clump of broken dried mud bricks she would sometime play under. They were still there only broken in more pieces than when she played with them. Looking at the tiny area she would cram her small body into Shelby let her mind wonder back to the final day the terror came and the night she fled into the jungle.

With her body squeezed among the broken bud bricks she played with her make believe stick figures and all the animals she adored from the jungle. From the time she was a three-year-old her mother would smile and tell her she had the soul of the animals. They did not seem to be afraid of her and many would let her come within touching distance. She never tried to do more than reach out her fingers and barely touch one for fear they would run away. For hours she could sit at the jungle's edge and make the sounds of the birds and the animals that inhibited the thick jungle just beyond her world and they would come.

This was were she was playing, among the mud bricks, when the ugly man with the scar on his face, the man she knew as Hernando Kling, knocked her only playmate's father to the ground. Then he picked him up and carried him up the road to the big house. Shelby was less than twenty feet away in her little hiding place when it happened; no others in the village saw what happened. Later in the day when her one playmate close to her age asked her if she had seen his father, she lied for she was afraid to say anything to him.

Shelby closed her eyes and leaned against the tree as she thought about the episode and the little playmate.

His name was Jesus Garride and he was one year older than she was. She watched him for an hour as he looked for his father, often turning to look towards the big house on the hill but not daring to climb the road to the house. You were not allowed to walk on that road, you were told they would shoot anyone walking to the top of the road.

She finally stopped watching her friend look for his father only when her mother called her to the shack. Shelby's breathing became labored as she leaned against the tree thinking of what she saw when she entered the small shack. At first she was surprised and delighted with what she saw. Her mother was standing in the center of the room holding the most beautiful white dress in the world.

"Here my little girl, I have this for you, you will look beautiful in it. And here, look I have white shoes with buckles on top for you to wear. But first you must take a bath, I have built a fire and heated water for you."

Shelby had stood spellbound as her mother smiled and held out the clothes. "Mother! Where did you get such beautiful things?"

"Later little one, we will talk later, now you much take your bath. I also have something else for you." Her mother held out a pink bar of soap that Shelby snatched from her hand and held to her nose. Such a delicious smell she had never before smelled.

"Momma, where did this come from?"

"Mr. King came all the way down here and gave it to me little one, just as he did the other things, now hurry you must be ready in an hour."

"Ready? Ready for what Momma? Am I going somewhere with you?"

"Yes dear, now go, go to the tub before the water cools, and use the soap all over, even on your hair."

The tears streamed down Shelby's face as she rolls the memories before her eyes of that afternoon and night. For the first time after that night Shelby found her self-sobbing, huge racking sobs shook her body as the memories continued.

"Now that you have yourself nice and clean little one put these new panties and stockings on." Shelby was smiling and laughing as her mother gave her each item and watched her as she put them on. Shelby could hardly stop from rubbing her hands over the smooth silk panties she was wearing. She had never had anything but rough wool clothing to wear and it felt wonderful to her skin. When she had all the new clothes on and her hair brushed to a beautiful shine her mother pulled out a small pink ribbon from her breast and tied it to her hair. Shelby twirled and danced and laughed as her mother held up a small broken piece of glass for her to see herself in.

"When are we going Momma? Where are we going? She said as she continued to smile and laugh and dance around her mother.

"Little one, I want you to listen to me, Mr. King is an important man, he gives all of us work and he pays us. If he did not pay us we would have no way to earn money for the bare necessities we buy from the village down river. Mr. King said it is time for you to come to the big house, and that you are now old enough for what he wants. We will walk together up the road to his house and then I will leave. You must be nice to him and do what he asks of you. Do you remember the terrible pain you had when you ran a stick through your foot one day while trying to climb a tree?

"Yes Momma, I remember."

"And do you remember how much pain it was when one of the men helped me pull it out?"

"Yes Momma, I remember."

"Little one, Mr. King might asks you to do something that will hurt for a little while but soon the pain will go away when your body gets use to it. You must promise me you will not fight or try and hit or bite him in anyway. Promise me child!"

"I promise you Momma. But what would Mr. King do that might hurt me?"

"I cannot say the words Shelby, but remember you have promised me." Shelby knew it was very important to keep her promise, because that was the first time she ever recalled her mother using her name when she spoke to her. Her Momma had never like the name Shelby but she could do nothing about it, except to protest in her own little way by never calling her by that name.

"Why are you crying and looking sad Momma? Did I say something wrong?"

"No little one, you have said nothing wrong. But try and remember I was not given a choice in what will be happening." The memories are as fresh at this very moment as they were that long time ago, Shelby realized as she watches her Momma and herself walk the long road to the top of the hill hand in hand into the court yard of the big house. Never before had Shelby been this close to the house and her heart was beating fast. She was excited in being in front of the big house but also frightened for what her mother had told her at the shack.

When they entered the courtyard Shelby saw the big ugly man with a scar holding her playmates father just as he had held her daddy four years ago. And the same questions were being asked by Mr. King each time the man screamed from having his arms pulled almost out of there socket. When they noticed the woman and child Mr. King said something to the man with the scar, which made him release the man. He than walked over to the woman and told her to go back home, he would take the girl into the house.

Her Momma leaned down and kissed her on the cheek and whispered again about the promise she had made. Then giving her a shove towards the man her Momma turned and walked back down the road to her shack.

Scar face reached out his hand and took Shelby's as he led her into the big house. Shelby's eyes were big as saucers as she walked down a long hall with beautiful white stones for a floor. The walls were painted different colors and great pictures were hanging everywhere. He led her into a large room full of overstuffed furniture, things she could not believe existed in this life. Releasing her hand he pointed to a large sofa and beside the sofa was a large pitcher of lemonade that he said she could drink. He then told her to sit there and wait until Mr. King came for her. Shelby turned to thank him as he stood there looking at her and her thanks stuck in her throat. The look in his eyes and his smile almost made her pee in her new panties. She quickly turned and sat on the big sofa as she was told and when she looked up again he was gone.

Chapter 12

Alex backed the truck down his driveway just after darkness, close to seven-thirty, and headed south on Rockwell Avenue, one of the major streets in Oklahoma City. In the back of the truck was his bicycle and helmet; he would use the bike to get back home without anyone thinking anything about seeing a man on a bike. He would use the bike and running trails running around Wiley Post Airport to get back to his house. Earlier he had taken the body from the truck and put him in the passenger's side of his small pickup. Buckled in and a baseball cap on his head he looked like any other person would look that was leaning back in his seat. Alex knew he could drop the body at the cemetery at Rockwell Avenue and N.W. 63rd street. A driveway was connected to Rockwell Avenue and he could pull in and drive down the small decline to the back of the cemetery where he would be almost out of sight of any one going by in a vehicle. It took him less than twenty seconds to hop out of the truck and open the passenger's side and lift the body out and place him behind the large stone less than five feet away. Someone would have to almost stumble on the body before they spotted it, but the maintenance people worked the grounds every few days and would spot him. Alex felt better knowing the man would be found and properly buried.

Driving down Rockwell Avenue Alex spotted the place he wanted to park the truck. It was a large parking lot at tenth and Rockwell. The large store occupying part of the grounds was Albertson groceries and most nights the lot was packed. That was what he was hopping he could do, to be able to pull a large truck into the lot without drawing a lot of attention. Once Alex had the truck parked in a far corner of the lot he dusted every thing inside the cab. Next he opened the back and took out his bike. He had already dusted everything in the truck before he left that evening. Closing and locking the doors Alex grabbed his helmet and took off down Rockwell until he came to the turn by the Bethany Medical Clinic. There he turned and cycled towards Lake Overholser where he picked up the riding trail that followed the boundaries of Wally Post Airport back to his house.

Back home Alex breathed a sigh of relief that he had actually gotten away with it. Now he needed sleep because tomorrow he would begin a quest he knew nothing about.

Bright and early, after a surprisingly good nights sleep, Alex was at the computer in his den goggling every thing he could find on money laundering, secret bank account, off shore accounts and anything else related to hiding large sums of money. He was amazed at the information he learned, for when he began the process he felt sure he would have to dig very deep to find anything useful, Christ, he found more than he could cram in his head. Within five hours he knew the avenue he would take, and he had chosen this one because it was fast. He had less than three months to do what he needed to do to get his company back and by God he would get his company back and teach his old partner a valuable lesson in ethics. Scratch that he laughed, I don't think I can teach him about ethics if I'm going to do what my plan calls for. Instead I'll just give him a lesson he will not forget.

Checking that his passport was still valid Alex made reservations for the British Virgin Islands for two days from today. Leaving a note for Vera stating he had found a lead in getting their company back and

Telling her he would be back in a week he packed two large suitcases, each with thirty million dollars in one hundred-dollar bills. Next using the same boxes from the truck he spent the next day going to four different U-Store buildings where he deposited four hundred eleven million, two hundred thousand dollars in each.

Alex had checked out each building before signing a contract, which they all required. But the four he went too paid no attention to what he wrote down nor did they ask for identification from him. That left only one more U-Store for the remaining four hundred eleven million, two hundred thousand dollars to be secured. This one was just down the road from his house on Rockwell Avenue between 63rd street and 50th street. Pulling in with his last load Alex parked the truck and walked to the front office. In case any of the U-Store places had asked for Identification Alex was dressed in his running clothes and if they had asked for any he could try and talk them out of it because he would say he had just gotten back from riding and forgot his wallet.

But as he had observed they had not even watched him sign the contract, the only thing they wanted was the cash he held in his hand for a year's contract. Holding the cash in his hand, he had called earlier to find out exactly how much it would be for a year at each location, he opened the door and went up to the clerk.

"Hi, I need to store some things for a year and I have the cash to pay for the full year." Alex said to the tall lankly man behind the counter.

Mo Pierce looked up at the man and then down at the cash before sliding an application towards Alex to sign.

"I'll need some identification when you finish the application." The tall man said as he turned his back and hit the keyboard on his computer. Alex froze, as he was about to put a fictitious name on the contract.

"Listen uh, Mo I left my wallet at home, you see I was going riding after this at the park."

"Sorry, but it's the law, we have to see some kind of identification before we can let you sign a contract, it's dumb I know but what can I say, it's the law."

Alex knew he didn't have the time to scout out another U-Store as he was leaving in the morning. Then he thought of something, he remembered he had taken the dead mans wallet and drivers licenses.

"Mo, I have my old driver's license from Texas in my glove compartment, would that work for you?"

"Mister I don't care what kind of identification it is as long as you show me something." Alex told him he would be right back as he turned and went out the door. Sitting in his truck he reached into the glove compartment and took out the man's wallet. Looking at the picture he knew he looked nothing like the picture on the licenses, maybe he could take the chance and give him the identification. He might not even look at it.

Returning to the office and making sure he had a year's cash in plain sight he gave the man the driver's license. As Alex filled out the contract he kept his eyes on the clerk who was imputing the information from the license into the computer.

When Alex finished the contract and gave it to the clerk along with the cash he was sure the man had not once looked at the photo. As the clerk handed him back his contract and his license he gave Alex a once over which did not set well with Alex. But there was nothing he could do now, and tomorrow he would be far away.

"Your drivers license is expired, did you know that Mr. Kling?" The man said as Alex was pushing the door open. Alex stopped and looked at his license.

"Damn, your right Mo, thanks for letting me know, I'll get it renewed when I get back to Texas."

Alex unloaded his cargo in the U-Store shed and locked it with a large lock that you would have to cut with a big wire cutter if you wanted in. glancing to the office as he drove out Alex saw that Mo was back in his chair reading a magazine.

Chapter 13

Shelby was having an argument with Captain Ruiz over the phone. He was of the same opinion as the Americans and their Director that the merchandise being talked about was a massive shipment of Heroin or Hash coming together in one area. Shelby did not agree.

"That's crazy Captain, why would they ship drugs into one central place, no one does that. Would you put all your eggs in one basket?"

"Well Agent Cruse, that's exactly what they did, put all there eggs in one basket, no matter what the merchandise is."

"Yes, I understand that Captain but not drugs. The merchandise has to be something else!"

"Doesn't matter Cruse, what ever it was they seemed to have lost it or one of them took off on his own with it. Keep your ears open, you're eyes are what we have at ground zero as you are the only one that can pick up outgoing calls at the moment. The American's are pissed because they lost contact with the outgoing traffic yesterday. So keep yourself alert, your next contact will be in three hours."

"Negative on that Captain, my main job will begin before that and I will be out of contact until I've completed the job."

"The hell you will Agent Cruse, your main job is to monitor the traffic until we say different, do not, I repeat, do not attempt to begin your secondary job until authority is given by either me or the Director."

"Understood Captain, will continue to observe and record until further notice."

Shelby clicked off and slammed the receiver back in its holder. God Damn it, she hated waiting for someone to give her orders, now she would have to recheck every square meter of the compound tomorrow just as she did today. This was something she did not want to wait on; she was itching to get into the compound and kill any thing that moved until she crossed his path. Then she would think about how she would kill him, maybe the same way he had killed her father. That thought sent a chilling wave of horror deep in her gut.

And another thing the target was confirmed in place, that might not be the case the next day. Shelby relayed that thought at the next contact time but it made no difference to the Captain. She was not to advance, but stay in place until further ordered.

The beeping in her ear would have awakened her if she had not already been awake at five forty-five the next morning. The beeping told her an outgoing call was being made from the house. She had been watching when the first rays of light peaked over the mountain, studying the compound and the comings and goings of each guard. They all had habits, some very bad habits that she would take advantage off when she entered the compound. Now she listened as the phone call was connected.

"Hello."

"Jack Strong please."

"Speaking."

"Good morning Jack, Hector King here. How is my Elizabeth?"

"Your Elizabeth is find Mr. King and she is ready to leave P.O. C. There was no problem, as you figured, with N.O.C."

"There has been a small complication Jack, you don't have a problem waiting a few days longer to do?"

"That will not be a problem Mr. King, you have taken care of your end of the business very generously. I can stay a few more days with Elizabeth, call me when you are ready."

"Thank you Jack, I will be in touch."

Shelby sent the message, than leaned back against the tree and played the conversation over in her mind.

Elizabeth! Who was Elizabeth? Was that a daughter? Where was she at the moment and why was this Jack

Strong taking care of her. And what about this poc and noc? What did they stand far? Shelby hit her transmission button and called Director Gozares. When she tried to call Captain Ruiz at the three-o'clock check in she had been transferred to the Director. She was than informed that Captain Ruiz was on another assignment and all future calls would come to him direct.

She was already pissed off with the way things were going on this assignment and this just made it worse. She trusted Captain Ruiz and knew he would give her the straight truth without any of the side menu's other agents seem to give, all in the name of protecting something or someone.

"Report Agent Cruse." The Director said as soon as he picked up the phone, no hello or nothing. Shit, she was getting to dislike the man more and more.

"Why was Captain Ruiz pulled away as my contact Director?"

"That's none of your business, Agent Cruse, what do you have to report?"

"I assume you got my transmission a few minutes ago, have you had time to analysis it?"

"Were working on it now."

"You have any ideas what poc and noc relate to?"

"Were working on it."

"Does Hector King have any children by the name of Elizabeth?"

"Were working on that."

"Gee Director, is there anything else you would like to tell me!"

"Keep your smart ass remarks to yourself Agent Cruse, your next report will be in three hours." He clicked off without another word.

Shelby felt the steam rising from her head, if he had been standing in front of her she would have killed him with her bare hands and enjoyed doing it. But she must keep calm so like the old warrior taught her Shelby took many deep breaths and stilled her mind and body until she felt herself becoming part of the forest. Than the quietness in her mind came and her body followed. For more than an hour, with one foot tucked under the cheek of her butt and the other barely touching the ground, she stood with outstretched arms as silent and still as the trees around her.

While in that state of mind Shelby broke apart the conversations and put them back together in a new light. When she saw what she needed she used her private cell phone and dialed the number put to memory. He answered on the second ring, also his private cell phone.

"Why are you no longer my contact?"

"I am unable to answer that, are you all right?"

"Yes, but things are not smelling right and I am not getting any cooperation from my new contact."

"I understand, but you know my hands are pretty much tied, why have you called me?"

"Because I need some answers, answers that I know will never come from him. I need your help, you have access to the computers."

"That might be a little difficult at the moment, I would have to access the mainframe."

"Mainframe! You're at headquarters?"

"Yes."

"Captain I need your help, like you needed mine in Cali." The Captain gave a deep sigh before speaking.

"I have often wondered when you would call that card in. Tell me what you need and I will call back in four hours. If you do not get the call you will know I have failed and will be either running or dead."

"Thank you."

"It must be very important to you to put yourself and me at such a high risk."

"It is Captain, I thought I would go to my grave without calling in that card."

"What is it you need, tell me now so I may get started."

"Pull the complete file on Hector King, the complete file Captain, not the one most people would receive. Than put in the computer poc and noc. Oh and just so someone else will know if anything happens to me, the merchandise they were talking about. It's not drugs at all, it's money."

Chapter 14

Alex and Vera had taken this trip two times in the last six years and no customs agent ever checked any of their bags. No one was concerned about bringing drugs in only with taking them out of the country into the United States. This would be the time though that his plans could go up in smoke if he was required to open either large suitcase he was dragging along behind him through the customs area in the British Virgin Island, where he had landed less than ten minutes ago.

With Sixty million in one hundred dollars bills in anyone's luggage would make a person's heart race while going through customs but Alex was remarkably calm. Maybe it was the other two billion fifty-seven million dollars hidden away at the U-Store buildings that kept his heart from racing or maybe he was becoming a thief after all.

The custom agent gave him a quick smile and motioned him on through into the bright sunshine. Alex hailed a cab and went directly to the bank he found on the Internet and whom he had spoken to less than five hours ago. He had a slip of paper with a name and the time he was to meet him at the bank. Alex reached the bank thirty minutes before the appointment and spied a Starbucks two stores from the bank. There he sat for the full thirty minutes watching the people go by and ordering one of the ice-coffee drinks found on the large cardboard menu leaning against the front wall.

Lying in front of him, with a leg propped on each, were the two large bags that people would have killed for if they knew what was inside each. Alex looked around at the people sitting and standing drinking there different drinks and he smiled. *How many of them are down here for the same reason I am here for* he thought. Two weeks ago he would never in his wildest dreams thought he would be sitting where he was getting ready to do what he was going to do. *Boy* he thought *your life can change in a second and you end up doing things you were against your whole life. What's the old saying? Some times in a persons life a door opens and you have to take a chance and walk through it. Well! He had sure as hell walked through that door and he would be walking through a lot of new doors in the next couple of months.*

At the precise time Alex walked through the side door to the bank that he had been instructed to do. He was glad he didn't have to tramp through the lobby of the bank wheeling two large bags with him. Heads would definitely have turned if he had done that.

Walking down the well-lit hall Alex knocked on the third door to his left and heard a female voice tell him to enter. Alex looked down at the piece of paper he had in his hand to make sure he read the instructions correctly. He had written down that he was to knock on the third door on the left and he had done that, but the female voice threw him. He was told he would be meeting a John Morgan. Opening the door half way Alex leaned his head in and looked at the person sitting at the desk. It was a woman between fifty -five and sixty-five and she was smiling at him.

"Mr. Jack Hitz?" That was the name Alex had given the man on the phone five hours earlier and whom he thought he had made the appointment with.

"I'm sorry, I was looking for John Morgan, I must have the wrong information."

"That's me Mr. Hitz, Jon Morgan."

"Jon! Oh, I see I must have written the name down wrong, but I thought I would be meeting with the man I had spoken to earlier today."

"No Mr. Hitz, he was the filter, the message was pasted on to me."

"Filter? I don't understand."

"Filter Mr. Hitz, what does a filter do? It stops things from going any further, right? I have no knowledge of the filter and he has no knowledge of you, other than the name you gave him this morning."

"I think I understand now, I'm not very good at this game."

"It's not a game Mr. Hitz, and if you believe it is we have no further business to discuss."

"Sorry, very poor choice of words. What I meant to say is that I have never been involved in anything like this before and I'm not sure what is the proper way to precede."

"I'll accept that Mr. Hitz. What we will do today is transfer your items into a special account with a special code for you to use any time you access the account. When we complete our transactions you may than give me any special instructions you need the bank to perform? As I'm sure you know but something I am compelled to state to you before we began, is that any item you transfer to this bank will not earn interest. Is that clear Mr. Hitz."

"I didn't know that, but it is not a concern of mine."

"Good, than Mr. Hitz what do you have in those two large bags that you wish to transfer to the our small bank?"

"Sixty million American dollars, all in one hundred dollar bills." Alex was watching her intently when he mentioned the amount to see the reaction he would get. To his surprise her facial expression did not change.

"Will the bank be the permanent depository of your funds Mr. Hitz or will there be transfers?"

"There will be transfers."

"And when will these transfers take place?"

"I will be in Switzerland in two days. I'm hoping the transfers can begin on the third day."

"Please do not discuss your details of where you're going Mr. Hitz. Will the transfers close out the account?"

"Heavens no! Only about half should be transferred, the remaining funds won't be needed for a couple of months, if at all." That caused a wide smile on the banker's face Alex noticed.

"Very well Mr. Hitz, now let's get down to the paper work, we want to make sure there is no money trail for someone to follow. I will not contact you in any way and you are never to try and contact me through the bank or anywhere else. Do you agree to that Mr. Hitz? Alex only nodded his head. Good, now one other thing Mr. Hitz, a matter of my fee, it will be one percent of the total account."

Again Alex only nodded but he hadn't thought about the fee before and when he calculated it in his head he was surprised it was so high, six hundred thousand dollars!

In less than an hour Alex was walking out the front door of the bank with the slip of paper and his code name and number. He would have been out sooner but the small machine in Jon Morgan's office could only count the money ten thousand dollars at a time. She mentioned to Alex he should memorize the name and the code numbers and then burn the paper they were written on.

Riding back to the hotel he had made reservations at Alex took each number, seven in all, and made a picture in his mind that had something to do with each number. When he had that down pat he thought of seven friends whose letters of there name added to the code. Too further cement the memory Alex put the names in alphabetic order. For example the first number was seven, and he knew a friend whose name was Alberts, first in the alphabetic plus seven letters to his name. The sixth number also was a seven and he remembered a friend's name that was Kempton. These were the only two duplicate numbers.

At the hotel Alex showered and order a large steak. By the time he had showered and eaten he had the codes down. He checked himself at least fifty times by writing his answers on a slip of paper and than checking it back to the slip he had received at the bank. The numbers were the only things he was concerned about, the name, Jack Hitz, he knew he would not forgot that name. It was the name of a friend in grade school that was killed in a bicycle accident. Alex was riding six to seven feet behind him when they tried to cross a busy road and his friend did not see the car coming. Alex stopped and shouted but it was to late, the car threw him more than a hundred feet and his head landed on a large rock. When Alex lifted the boy's head he could see that part of his brain was left on the rock, his friend lived until the next morning. For months after that Alex would be playing football with other friends and the dead boys face would take the place of the friend he was trying to tackle. The first time it happened Alex freaked out when he saw the face; just as he flew threw the air to tackle the boy carrying the ball. The kid ran over him like a Mack truck and almost knocked him out because Alex dropped his arms when he saw the face.

Chapter 15

Dusk was just beginning to fall when the phone call came. Shelby felt the vibration and pulled her private phone from her breast pocket and spoke.

"What do you have for me?"

"What! No hello or I love you?"

"Cut the shit Captain and give me what you have."

"Elizabeth did not refer to his daughter or anyone else in his family. Elizabeth is a ship, a yacht to be exact. A small but very swift yacht, the last reported location was seventeen days ago as it exited the Panama Canal going west."

"A yacht! What the hell is he doing talking about his yacht and asking if it's in------place. Anything else interesting in the computers about him?"

"No, I had to get out three times fast, someone noticed my intrusion each time but I'm sure I cut the link before they could trace me. The fourth time I got a little more creative, I was in the director's office a couple of months ago and I picked up his password. I had been dismissed and was opening the door to leave when I remembered something else I needed to discuss with him. He had turned his back to me and was entering his password as I approached him. When I realized what I had seen I quickly stepped back to the door and made like I was coming back in. I wasn't sure if he still had the same password, everyone is suppose to changed them every thirty days but knowing how confident he was I figured the rules never applied to him. Apparently I was right. I finally got the information with his password but there was very little else in King's file. When I used the mainframe to crunch poc and noc the only hit I got that would have anything to do with a ship was the noc letters."

"And the computer said what about the noc letters?"

"That they could be abbreviations for New Orleans Customs."

"Nothing at all for the poc letters?"

"Sure, hundreds of suggestions but nothing that I could see had anything to do with King or his yacht."

"You still remember what I said about the merchandise?"

"Yep, but I don't know what that would have to do with his ship, you don't ship money, if that's what it is, through the waters of America. Doesn't make since, you would transport the money just like he was doing, by truck. If it is money there must be one hell of a lot of it. You think he is trying to laundry it in the Houston area?"

"Why would he bring five separate loads of cash to one area? And if he did, why would it be in Houston, that's not a money capital. There's something buzzing around in my head and I can't pinpoint it, keep your private phone with you. I'll be in contact."

"Are you keeping secrets from be now? I hear things in your voice that you're not saying."

"No Captain, I'm not, you will be the first I tell if I do find anything."

"Keep in contact."

"Affirmative and I do love you Captain-----like a big brother."

Shelby leaned against the tree, closing her eyes she listened to the old warriors voice telling her to empty her mind, become one with the wind, water, smells and the forest surrounding her. His hands touching each of her young shoulders, hands that felt so soft to the touch but which she knew could turn to steel and crush a mans nose straight into the brain. She had been beside him, fighting for their life in waist deep water, when she witnessed the force of one quick jab to the attacker's face.

Emptying her mind she let the thoughts swirl by. Money, ship, transportation, New Orleans Customs, there was a connection here, she could feel it. Why did he call and ask if the ship was ready? Where is the ship now? It was heading west two weeks ago; it could be almost anywhere by now. West, west, what's in that direction?

Pulling out the small handheld computer Shelby typed in instructions for Map Quest and the Panama Canal, when that came up she expanded the map west until it hit Florida. Finally she hit the expand button to bring in the complete United States and then she sat staring at the tiny screen. Her eyes moved up and down the east cost of America looking for a place the ship might want to dock or a good place to run and hide. Running her eyes over the coastline of North America again and again they finally stopped on Houston as she sat almost in a dream state.

The call said the two carrying the merchandise never made it to Houston, where were they coming from? Who ever it was changed the plans for a lot of people. From information picked up she knew there were four shipments coming from different parts of the country, all converging somewhere close to Houston and she knew it had to be money. They would not do that with drugs because, as she told Captain Ruiz, it just did not make since.

Why bring that much money into one place? Why not disburse it in all the major cities of America, they could laundry the money so much easier. All right, they want the money in one place, what for? What can you do with millions of dollars? Buy someone or some company off? No! Not with that amount of cash, something much bigger is at stake.

Think Cruse, damn it, think! It's there tucked away in your mind you can feel it. Agent Shelby scanned the coast again from Houston east to Florida and back again towards Houston. Her eyes swept past New Orleans, stopped and returned to the half-drowned city. Something, something, something, what the hell is it Cruse. Was the ship coming to or through New Orleans? If so-------Shelby punched in information for United States Customs than for New Orleans Customs. Punching in the register of the yacht, Elizabeth, she got a hit. Hot damn Shelby said with a big grin. New Orleans Customs inspected and logged the Elizabeth through six days ago.

Shelby studied the New Orleans area before expanding the map to take in all of Louisiana, Arkansas and Oklahoma. She followed the highways and byways north, nothing registered but when her focus shifted east to west she spotted the poc mentioned in the phone conversation my King and the man taking care of the yacht. Poc stood for Port of Catoosa and that was what had been rattling around in her head from the time she heard King mention poc.

She shook her head several times castigating herself for not coming up with poc sooner. She knew she should have, Jordan Daniels, the F.B.I. instructor who early on became her mentor while she was training at their facilities used a training exercise that went right through that area. The exercise included a phase where she was tracking a shipment of radioactive material off loaded at the Tulsa, Oklahoma airport. Four teams were given the same assignment as they stepped off the plane at the Tulsa airport. Shelby was assigned to the team in which Jordan Daniels was the observer. Each team included a senior F.B.I. Agent that did nothing but monitor the progress of the team, he was not allowed to give advice.

A trickle of information was fed to each team by phone calls from people they did not know. On other occasion's, if they interpreted the information correctly it would lead them to a person who knew or might know something about the shipment and who might or might not have something in his possession that would reflect this. It was from these people that Shelby found the information she needed. In Jordan Daniels final report on the training exercise he mentioned, among other things, that that was where her true skill of observation came in. she was able to differentiate between the lies some of the men said and the truth. She picked up small details that every one else missed and when shown the clues after the exercise many of the agents still could not see them until actually pointed out by the instructor.

The final clue lead her far away from her training partners whom refused to believe some of the things she was telling them. While they were still in Tulsa searching the truck lines and cross country bus lines she had been squatting all night in the shadows of the Port of Catoosa and when the small van backed up to the docks where a tug with two barges waited she struck. Both men in the van were neutralized the moment they stepped to the back of the van. Pulling off the jacket of one of the men lying on the ground and grabbing the hat from the other she carried the container they had delivered straight down the gangplank and up to the wheelhouse where three men were waiting. As soon as she stepped into the wheelhouse she fired her laser gun and a red dot appeared in the center of the foreheads of two men. There was no movement from the third man as she exited the tug carrying her cargo, which she plopped in the lap of the man she had taken the hat from. Next she took of the jacket and laid it at the feet of the man she had taken it off of. Then she took off the hat and with a smile placed it on the second mans head as she watched from the corner of her eye the approach of Jordan Daniels.

"Why?" Was all he said when he stood in front of her but she knew what he was referring too; she smiled and said.

"Because he was one of yours."

"How did you know the third man was ours?"

"Because he saw me as I reached for the door and he gave no reaction to my present."

"And if he had?"

"I would have killed him through the window before opening the door, the other two had their backs to the door and would not have turned around before I was inside." Shelby reached down and helped up the man she had taken the hat from and he only shook his head in amazement that she had caught them so flat footed.

Shelby had to smile thanking back on that memory. It was a wonderful time training with the best in the world at what they do, but there was something missing in each of them when she got to know them better, something within themselves. The old warrior had given her skills for survivor and without them she would have failed a long time ago, these men were never put into the kinds of situations as young boys that would cause them to live or die on a decision.

Shelby traced the map with her finger beginning at the Port of Catoosa on the outskirts of Tulsa. It was called the McClellan-Kerr Navigation system, in Oklahoma, and it was built in the sixties so that product could be shipped from Oklahoma, Arkansas and Louisiana all the way to the Port of New Orleans.

The Elizabeth was now docked at Catoosa outside of Tulsa or at lease it was at the time of the last conversation she heard from Mr. King. The missing truck, and at this point she knew she needed to be thinking about a large truck, because of the other four being mentioned as trucks, was suppose to be heading for Houston but never made it. The yacht is docked in Catoosa waiting for something or someone. Pulling her finger down close to Houston see looked at the highways going in all directions. But only one was heading in the direction of Oklahoma. Highway 45 was heading straight up where it would connect with I-35 straight to Oklahoma City and then a turnpike to the Port of Catoosa and the waiting ship.

They're waiting for the truck to arrive at the Port; they're taking the money down river and out to sea. There going to laundry the money overseas, a lot less security in the Old Russian States, would be ease to laundry that much money. *I'll be damn she laughed, Mr. King your cutting out your partners. Including the one that made the phone call telling you the shipment was missing. To bad you won't be able to enjoy all that money; you have an appointment with me as soon as darkness comes. She didn't gave a damn what Director Gozares orders were, it was time for Mr. King to die.* With that Agent Shelby squatted and waited for the hunt, something she had done many times before.

Five minutes before she started down the hill towards the big house Agent Shelby sent a message to Jordan Daniels her old mentor with the F.B.I.

Chapter 16

Alex waited at the gate watching the passengers debark from the KLM flight 17 from England to Switzerland. He spotted Vera as soon as she made the turn in the tunnel, Alex decided two days ago on his arrival in Switzerland that he could not go on deceiving Vera about what he was doing. Instead of trying or even wanting to tell her over the phone when he called her he had only told her he needed her there with him and for her to look in the middle drawer of his chest cabinet under the sweaters but only after he hung up. What she found under the sweaters was one neatly wrapped packaged of one hundred-dollar bills that totaled one hundred thousand dollars. Vera loved Alex and trusted him with her life but after counting the money she was frightened that he had committed a crime and the only way to know for sure was to meet him when and where he had suggested. The place she was meeting him was not a good sign Vera knew for she knew enough about extradition to know that could be the reason he was there. The United States would have a very hard time getting him back home.

Vera was not smiling when she hugged Alex but she looked deep into his eyes and told him she loved him. Alex waited until they were back at the hotel before he mixed her a strong drink and told her to find a conformable chair.

"I don't need a conformable chair Alex and I don't need this drink I only need you to tell me what kind of trouble your in and see if we can get you out of it. I haven't practice law in over twenty years Alex, but that doesn't mean I haven't kept up with my profession."

"I should have waited until you came back from your mothers or at lease called you when it happened but I think you will understand my state of mind when it happened. The day you left, or was it the day after you left, oh well it doesn't matter. Anyway I was running my usual route when I came across a large moving van parked half on the street and half on the grass with a man standing by the open drivers door. When I made my turn and came back to pass the truck I glanced over and notice the man was half lying in and half out of the truck."

"I stopped to see if he needed help and when I got close I could see he was unconscious and his head was hanging off the seat. When I pulled him up I saw that his face was gray, and he was trying to tell me something. Finally he got out that he was having a heart attack and needed me to get his pills out of the glove compartment. After fumbling around I finally located the pill and put it under his tongue and in a minute or two he started getting better so I told him I was calling nine-one-one. But he stopped me, saying he only needed to rest for a few hours and could I take him to our house. When I hesitated and told him he really needed an ambulance he reached into a sack and drew out ten thousand dollars and gave it to me. I tried to refused but he kept insisting and I finally agreed."

"He gave you ten thousand dollars just to take him home with you to rest for a few hours!"

"Honest to God Vera that's what happened."

"There was one hundred thousand dollars under your sweaters, not ten thousand!"

"I know, I know! Will you let me finish please; I drove the truck home and parked in back. When I turned off the truck and looked over his face was gray again. I laid him down in the truck and tried to find a pulse but couldn't find any. I gave him mouth to mouth but there was nothing I could do to help him, he was dead. I was sitting there trying to think what I should do when I spotted the bag he had taken the ten thousand from so I looked inside and found another forty thousand dollars wrapped in one hundred bills just like the first packet."

"You didn't think about going to the police about that time Alex, you had a dead man and fifty thousand dollars. Didn't it ever come to your mind that the man might have stolen the money?"

"Of course it did Vera, nobody offers ten thousands dollars to rest for a few hours in your home but when I was sitting there think it all through It also made me curious about what he had in the back of the moving van."

"I think that was an easy call Alex, you're going to tell me when you looked in the back you found marijuana bags, right?"

"That's the same thing I thought of Vera." Alex said as he looked at her before continuing.

"It wasn't drugs?"

"No."

"The hundred thousand dollars under your sweater, you found that in the truck?'

"Yes and more."

"And more what? More money, you found more than one hundred thousand dollars?"

"I found the truck full of boxes, all were three feet by three feet by two feet. All wrapped with clear plastic tape." Vera was frowning and shaking her head as he described the boxes.

"For Christ sake Alex, what was in the boxes?"

"Money."

"Money! There was money in all the boxes? How much money Alex?" Alex had been turning a white sheet of paper over and over in his hand while they were talking and when she asked that question Alex turned it toward her with the numbers written in black.

"Two million one hundred thousand----two hundred million-----two billion! Come on Alex your telling me there was two billion, one hundred seventeen million dollars in the boxes?"

"That's what I'm telling you Vera."

"Oh my God Alex! That's drug money."

"I know, but it was like God sent it to me because of what happen with Chuck Witt and our company."

"Cut the crap Alex God didn't send you that money, that money is so dirty you could never clean it. And what do you think the people that lost the money are doing right now. Sitting around moaning about their loss?"

"I know what there doing Vera and I know how powerful they are but I think I covered the trail pretty good and dispersed the money in a number of places. Remember it was early in the morning and still dark, no one was on the street and when I parked the truck in the back. And then when I pulled it around into the building I know no one saw me."

"Alex they will hunt for you until they die and than their partners will continue the hunt. We have to go to the police with this before they find us!"

"Vera, listen to me, we have an opportunity that will never come again. Let me tell you what I want to do and as soon as we get the company back we'll call the police from some pay phone and tell them where to get all the money. I'll even put back the amount I took out of the country three days ago." Vera decided she needed that drink after all as she leaned back in the chair and listened to what her husband was planning to do. When he was finished she strongly disagreed with what he would do but told him she would be by his side, no matter what happened. Her only stipulation was that the children would never know about it and they were never to be involved in case the wrong people found out about whom had the money.

Vera was the one that took the lead to form the contracts for the different dummy corporations so that when the money was transferred it would be almost impossible to trace where it came from. Unless a number of governments corroborated and that was highly unlikely after Vera ran the companies through a dozen different countries in Europe and Asia. Once that was done the transfer of the first thirty million dollars flowed from one company to another. Some companies keeping a part of the funds and sending the rest on to another company. Three weeks later another twenty-five million dollars was transferred in another direction to the same companies. Once that was done each company began buying the stock of the bank that held the notes on Alex's company. In another three weeks fifty-one percent of the bank was owned by the companies controlled by Alex and Vera. Now all Alex had to do was wait for the finally meeting with his old partner, Chuck Witt, and hand him a cashier's check for a little over one million dollars instead of it being the other way around.

Chapter 17

The crescent moon rose over the jungle as Shelby advanced down the mountain keeping the small village close to her right. Her passing was so silent and swift that even the night jungle animals were not aware of her presence. An hour later she stood silently beside the little shack she had called home for eight years and from which she fled in terror on an almost moonless night such as this night. She could hear the heavy breathing of an older male, a younger woman and a small child inside the shack. Her feet itched to move from this place but her mind held her fast until a slow moving cloud obscured what was left of the half crescent moon. As the moon vanished she stepped from the shadows and silently raced up the dirt and rutted road to the top of the hill.

The guard was fifteen yards in front of her smoking a cigarette; his M16 was across his back. There would be three guards on the outside of the wall, this one at the corner of the south wall, one at the other corner of the south wall and the third standing by the south gate going into the middle of the court yard. Thinking of the conversation she was about to have with King, Shelby's pulse was beating hard; she could hear the blood in her ears as it raced from her heart. The old warrior's words came softly to her. *Before the battle begins feel the gently wind on your back and the warm morning sun upon your face, let your heart and your mind feel this presence as it steadies your soul.*

Shelby breathed deeply a dozen times as her heart rate declined with each breath until her pulse hovered around fifty and there it would stay until the battle was over. Too much Adrenaline, too many quick steps and the strength would be drained at the time you would need it the most. Circling to the right of the guard Shelby reached the west wall and walked in its shadow until she was three feet behind the right shoulder of the first guard. He had finished his cigarette and was standing with his back at the end of the south wall with only the right one third of his body beyond the wall. The M16 was still strapped to his back and was pressed against the wall where he stood.

Shelby brought her left fist, with the middle knuckle extended, level with her shoulder and in one blinding thrust made contact at the base of the guards neck; at the same time her right hand shot out and cover his mouth. The only thing the guard saw was the brilliant little lights going off in his brain as his spine was disconnected from his brain stem, he felt no pain as she caught his fallen body and lowered it to the ground against the west wall.

Now Shelby had to be fast for she needed to circle the big house to where the east wall connected to the south wall where the second guard was standing. She figured she had less than two minutes before the guard at the gate realized the guard on his right was missing. If she were lucky the guard would think he had stepped around the building to relieve himself and that would give her another couple of minutes before he would become suspicious.

Looking at her watch as she stood less than ten feet behind the second guard she saw that ninety seconds had elapsed from the start of her operations. Staying in the shadow of the wall she studied the guard for ten more seconds before deciding to use the same move she had on the first guard. Five quick steps would bring her within striking distance as she made her move. On her fourth step and as she was coiling her right arm for the strike, something made the man turn in her direction. Without hesitation, instead of the base of his spine as the target, she struck and crushed his windpipe at the same time her left hand grabbed the front of his jacket and pulled him back from the corner. Making gagging noise's, with his hands in front of his neck he went down to his knees. As he fell to his knees Shelby stepped behind him, put one hand against his right ear and the other hand on his jaw than she gave a short powerful jerk and broke the mans neck.

Two minutes and twenty seconds into the operation Shelby peered around the corner of the south wall to see what the third guard was doing. He was walking towards the first guards position with his M16 at ready, that surprised Shelby, it also told her he was one notch up on the guard scale, which determined her next move. Running silently she closed the gap between them as she reached behind and pulled out the small black silencer that she screwed to the end of her M11/9 Cobray. She was fifteen feet behind him with her gun at waist level when he heard her and began to turn. Shelby squeezed the Cobray trigger for only a microsecond and five bullets spit out the end of the silencer. The first two went just below his left shoulder blade; the third went through the middle of his back and exploded in his heart, the fourth and fifth hit just under the right shoulder blade and punctured one lung. The impact threw the man to the corner of the building and his body rested less than four feet from the first guards body.

Five minutes later Shelby had concealed all three bodies to where no one would stumbled upon them in the middle of the night if they happen to be checking on them. Standing in the shadows by the front gate to the courtyard Shelby watched silently for twenty minutes, her pulse still beating under fifty. Not a muscle moved as she stood like a statue taking everything in. She was satisfied with the operations so far, although she had to use a gun on the third guard she knew it was necessary. She preferred using only her hands; it was close and personal, not cold, as it is with a weapon and even more important hands never misfire or jammed. And sometimes in close quarters guns are a handicap that can get you killed by a skilled foe that relies on his or her hands while you're trying to use the gun.

Shelby could not detect one single guard in the courtyard and that disturbed her. King would not have allowed the courtyard to be unguarded unless he was not here. But he had to be she thought no plane or car left in the time she was watching. Opening the gate and moving silently through the courtyard Shelby encounter no guards, only when she reached the inter walkway did she hear voices. Keeping her M11/9 Cobray at her side she moved toward the voices until she was inches from the window looking into the large kitchen. Three guards sat playing cards and drinking coffee, their guns leaning against the table. One woman in her forty or fifties was putting butter in a frying pan with beans and bacon she had been cooking and did not notice Shelby as she opened the door until she quietly asked where Hector King was.

As she opened the door and spoke all three guards looked up in surprise and reached for their guns. The silence bullets from Shelby's M11/9 Cobray found their targets before a single man had both hands on their gun. The woman dropped the wooden spoon she was using and turned toward Shelby moving her right hand to the small of her back, but another burst from the Cobray almost cut her in half. Listening for any noise or running feet Shelby waited full thirty seconds before approaching the woman. The woman had landed face down on the floor and in the small string of her apron was a Colt automatic.

Chapter 18

The vibration coming from her buttoned breast pocket told her she was receiving an incoming text message. Ignoring the message Shelby inserted another clip in the M11/9 Cobray and advanced down the hall to a large living room. Sweat was beginning to roll down her back as she stepped into familiar surroundings; the massive couch was still in the same place with the same ugly color she remembered from a long time ago. Trying to free her mind from the images flashing across the eyes of a nine year old she pulled the cell phone out and looked at the message scrolling across. The message read, *'Do not proceed with second goal, I repeat, do not proceed with second goal, Paul Gozares.'*

Shelby barred her teeth as a low growl escaped her throat as she read the message. Jabbing at the numbers with lightning speed Shelby replied. 'Second operation all ready in progress, Agent Cruse.' Shelby knew she had now burned the bridge back to her department and that she might even become a target herself, but that mattered little to her at the moment as she stealthily maneuvered her way down the different hall ways in the big house. No one else was found in her search as she hesitated at a pretty blue door that had been painted with a fresh coat of paint in the near past, her hand inches away from the handle.

Unable to control her thoughts, they came flooding back of that time long ago when she was a small innocent nine year old girl in a pretty white dress. She was setting on the big sofa waiting for someone to come and get her as the big man with the scar told her they would. Shelby had finished two big glasses of lemonade and it was beginning to take effect, she had to go pee but the man said to stay there. The large clock on the wall told her she had been sitting for more than an hour and she couldn't hold it much longer.

Fifteen more minutes Shelby sat on the couch squirming hoping the man would come back so she could go pee. When Shelby knew she could not hold it much longer she got up from the couch and repeated a number of times that she had to go to the bathroom. When she did not receive a reply she walked to the hall and looked out. First she walked down the hall to the right but found nothing that looked like a bathroom. Turning she walked the full length of the hall the other way and still did not find what she was looking for.

Needing urgently to find the bathroom Shelby followed the stairs down one story and opened four doors before she found the bathroom. Coming out of the bathroom she turned the wrong way and found herself completely lost in the maze of the level she was in. she backtracked a number of times to try and find her way back to the stairs but only proceeded to get more lost than before. Turning one corner she thought she remembered she walked past a door she had not noticed before. It was a pretty blue door and she wondered why she had not noticed such a pretty door before. Causally opening the door Shelby found she was standing by another stairs leading down. This stairs was beautiful, it was made of all marble, the most beautiful white marble Shelby had ever seen. The banister felt smooth and cold as she took her first few steps down. When she reached the bottom a short hall lead to another stairs descending down even further and this one to was all white marble. Smiling at the smoothness and the cold of the marble Shelby straddled the banister, pulling the front of her pretty white dress up so it would not get dirty as she slid down. Shelby laughed as she began to go quite fast and she had to squeeze the banister with her hands to slow down but than she hit something slick just before she came to the bottom and she flew off the end of the banister and landed on her back. She cracked her head as she hit and the stars flew from her eyes for a few seconds before she tried to get up. Brushing the wetness from her hands that she thought was water, against her dress Shelby looked back up the stairs at the slick spot. Something had spoiled the color of the marble both on the banister and each step all the way down from the first slick spot. Someone had splashed paint on the beautiful marble, red paint.

Shelby realized she had brushed her hands against the front of her dress and she quickly looked down at what was once a beautiful cloth belt but that was now streaked with red. Tears burst from her eyes as she saw other streaks of red on the front of her dress and when she pushed her fingers together the red paint was sticky between her fingers. Realization than came quickly for Shelby, the red paint wasn't paint at all, it was blood and she screamed at the same moment she heard another scream farther down the stairs.

Putting a hand over her mouth, Shelby sat on the cold marble floor and heard the scream again. It was a terrible scream, the sounds she had witnessed at the fringes of the jungle when one animal was in the process of killing another animal and the dying animal knew it was about to die. Wiping her hands on the marble banister to get most of the blood off Shelby started down the stairs in the direction of the scream. Three times before she reached the landing on the next floor she heard the scream, each time the scream became a little weaker.

Shelby had walked but a few steps when a door to her right was slightly opened and she heard voices beyond. Slowly opening the door Shelby saw she was entering a small balcony with delicate silk curtains covering the opening. The voices were getting louder as she crept close to the curtain and slowly pulled one of them away. Shelby's eyes became as big as saucers as she gazed down on two gigantic swimming pools. The waters in both a deep blue green, the pools covered most of the room, each were more than a hundred feet long.

By the first pool she saw beautiful chairs and tables with large fluffy towels hanging from the back of the chairs. It was so beautiful that Shelby had a hard time taking her eyes from the scene for she saw dolls some as large as little girls. And there were dollhouses and a number of tea sets on different tables. A wonderful place for a little girl to play and have fun when she finished her swimming. But she finally pulled her eyes away while pulling the curtain even further back until she saw where the voices were coming from. At first she thought the three men were playing a swimming game. One man was holding onto a rope as he hung over the clear blue green water that was foaming just below his feet, while the other two men stood approximately three feet behind and beside him.

Chapter 19

Shaking the memories from her mind Shelby pulled the blue door open and looked down at the marble stairs and hesitated before taking the first steps always keeping her hand off the banister. The memories almost overwhelmed her as she remembered the banister slide and the blood so much blood over all that beautiful white marble. Closing her eyes and taking a deep breath Shelby could almost hear the screams coming from that long past time. Slowly descending until she reached the small balcony she had entered so long ago. The fluffy silk curtains had been replaced with plain cotton drapes now. Of course they had to be replaced, she had touched them and smeared his blood when she had opened the curtains. Hearing no voices or movements beyond Shelby used the barrel of her M11/9 Cobray to move the curtain aside. The pools where still there with the same blue green water she had witnessed before that looked so inviting. The pretty dolls and all the other pretty things were still there. The devise still hung from the ceiling at the second pool as Shelby used every ounce of her strength to control her emotions and her memories. But it did no good as the memories flooded back from that terrible dark night so long ago, she slid to the floor and put a hand to her mouth as her eyes and memories played out like a movie.

Holding on to the devise descending from the ceiling was Jesus Garrido father. He was the young playmate who had searched for his father. The father that Shelby had seen being kicked and dragged to the big house and who she and her mother had seen again when her mother lead her to the inter courtyard earlier that day.

Watching the man she realized he was not holding into the devise, he was tied to it. And now she knew where all that blood on the stairs came from. They had dragged and pushed him down those beautiful white marble steps, his feet and hands bleeding as he tried to hold onto the banister as he was being kicked from behind. His hands tied above his head and each foot tied to a metal rod coming from the attachment above his head. His feet were tied a foot apart and Shelby tried not to look at the nakedness of the man but she could not help it. Mr. King was asking him questions and he was repeating the same answer, that he had told no one of the shipment. Each time he repeated the same answer the big man with the ugly scar, Hernando Kling, would touch him with a round stick and Jesus Garrido father would scream.

Shelby watched at Hernando Kling walked with the round stick back to a small box sitting on a chair and do something with a round knob, than he would walk back and touch the man again. Once when he did Shelby saw a puff of blue smoke come from the end of the round stick and saw that the stick had left a small black mark on the mans buttock. Mr. King would again ask the same question and the man would give the same answer and the man with the ugly scar would touch him again and he would scream again. Shelby realized that was the same question Mr. King had asked her daddy before they dragged him away to the big house on the hill. *This is where they took her daddy; they had done the same thing to him that they were doing to her friend's daddy. She began to cry thinking about her daddy, a daddy that never came back to her, why were they hurting this man and what did they do to her daddy.*

She wanted to run and hide but knew she had to stay to find out what happened to her daddy for she knew they were doing the same thing to her friends dad that they did to her daddy. The questions went on and on and Shelby almost fell asleep a number of times only to be jolted awake by his screams. Shelby watched as Mr. King took out his knife and cut the back of the man's leg, this was something new and she paid close attention to what they were saying.

"I'm tired of this game your playing Garrido, I trusted you with a very important assignment and you failed me, now you lie to me and you will pay with your life. Hernando will lower you slowly into the water until you talk or you die, which will it be?"

"I have told you the truth, I told no one, I do not know how they found out about the shipment, I swear on my mother's grave, I told no one!"

Shelby thought they were going to lower him into the pool until he drowned until she noticed the foam and bubbles and the churning of the water below his feet. Each time a drop of blood from his cut hit the clear blue green water the churning of the water would began again and it took Shelby but a few seconds to realize what was in the water. For she had seen them many times with her daddy when they would go to the stream to fish. Her daddy would take a small net and a piece of rope made from tree bark down to the edge of the stream. From the net he would put a small animal he had caught that morning and tie the rope around it's neck before using his knife to make a small cut in the side of the animal. Just enough to make it bleed but not enough that it would lay still when lowered into the water. He wanted the animal to struggle and spread the blood so the fish could smell it.

Shelby knew what these fish could do and she knew the name. Piranha, this was the most savage fish in the jungle streams and when it smelled blood it would attack in-groups to tear the flesh from anything it caught bleeding in the stream. In less than minutes the animal would be nothing but bones, every piece of flesh and fur would be consumed. Her daddy would do this and when the swarm started he would scoop his net down into the water and pull up ten to fifteen. They tasted very good, she thought they were the best tasting of all the fish but she did not like the way her daddy caught them.

No matter how much the man struggled he could do nothing from stopping his toes and than his feet from entering the water. She could barely stand the screams of agony coming from her friend's daddy as his feet were torn to shreds before the bones of his feet were pulled above the water. The Piranha's were leaping from the water trying to find the source of all the blood coming from what was left of his feet. The blood poured from his feet into the pool as the water was churned to froth by the Piranha's feverish attack on every drop of blood hitting the water.

When the man gave the same answer he had given for the last hour Hector King motioned to Hernando Kling and Shelby watched in utter horror as the man was lowered until his testicles reach the water and the Piranha's consumed half his body. Shelby saw her daddies' face as the man screamed for the last time and she screamed with him. Both men looked up to see the small child standing with her hands to her mouth starring at them.

Shelby turned screaming as she ran from the balcony and up the long stairs to the house above. Blinded with tears and panic she somehow found the right door that took her to the central courtyard and out the front gate. The two guards at the gate had their guns ready when they heard the screams and the doors slamming shut before they saw the child running directly towards them. The guard closest to her as she tried to run through the gate reached out and tripped her as she came flying by. She lay sprawled on her back as the two guards looked down at the blood smeared face of the little nine year old girl. Than they saw the bloody thighs and panties stained in red and they turned shameful eyes away thinking they knew what had happened at the hands of their boss, Hector King. They knew of many young pretty girls that had been left in the courtyard never to be seen again. And they both thought the same; 'maybe this little one can get away before he knows she is missing.' They turned their back on her as she scrambled to her feet and ran towards the jungle away from the big house.

For two days Shelby lived three to four hundred feet inside the jungle watching and fearing they would come for her for what she had witness. Hunger on the third day drove her to seek shelter in the small thatched house her mother occupied. Waiting until darkness she made her way to the back of the house and waited to hear any sign of movement from anyone around. The entire village was quite, far to quite she knew but she was too hungry to stay away. Sliding in the opening to her house Shelby crouched low and stayed silent until her eyes adjusted to the blacker darkness inside the hut. She could not hear her mother breathing but she knew she was there, for she could finally make out the outline of her lying on the bed. Crawling on her hands and knees she crept to her mother's side and whispered to her. Her mother did not reply as Shelby reached out to touch her face but her hand hit something hard as she brushed her hand above her mother's chest.

Looking back at what her hand had struck she could barely make out a large object protruding from her mothers chest and than she screamed as she saw what it was. At the same time she screamed a flashlight from the corner of the room came on and she heard him say.

"I knew the third night would be the night you would be coming back. The third night always gets them, they can stand the hunger for two days but not the third if they think there is food and safety. Mr. King believes you ran off into the jungle and died, I knew better, I've seen the fire in your eyes little one, you don't give up easy." Shelby watched as he struck a match to the lantern he was carrying and soon the small hut was lit and she could see who it was and that he was naked. She already knew who he was, the one with the ugly scar, and he was coming towards her with his thing, pink and big swinging back and forth and getting bigger the closer he came to her.

"For once I will be the first instead of him, always shoving them torn and bleeding to me when he is finished. Not this time little one, this night I will know what it's like to be the first and you will know what it's like to be with a man."

Shelby knew exactly what scar face meant, she had listened to her mother and father when she was very small and she had watched the animals doing it at the edge of the jungle. Shelby rolled on her back and smiled at him, which caused him to stop and cock his head as he looked down on her. Than he smiled as he began to bend his legs so he could reach down and tear off her bloody panties, as he touched her panties she struck out with the heal of her foot and caught him on his testicles pushing one back into his stomach cavity.

It was such a shock to his system that he expelled only a soft groan as he fell to his knees in front of her before toppling over on his side. Shelby raced for the door with only one quick glance at her mother lying on the bed with a machete imbedded in her chest. She ran and ran until she could run no more through the jungle, when morning came she had no idea where she was, she had no food and no weapons to defend herself. For two days she wondered before falling exhausted beside a small stream. She knew if she did not get up and try to find food that she would die in that spot. And that she could not do, not until she avenged her mother and her father and her small friend. Finding a sharp rock and location a log going across the small stream

Shelby stood on the log in the middle of the stream and used the rock to make a small cut in one finger which she than held over the water and waited. In less than a minute a mass of fish, Piranha, was swarming around each drop of blood from her finger. Squatting on the log Shelby steadied her body before swiftly reaching in with both hands and at the same time scooping upward towards the bank and threw whatever made contact with her hands. Five times she dipped her hands and scooped, each time one or two Piranha landed on the bank still gashing with the two rows of thirty needles like teeth at the air.

Twice as she scooped and threw a Piranha held fast to one of her fingers as it had bitten to the bone. Climbing off the log with two fingers that had long gashes she scooped up mud and mixed it with moss that she made into a paste. She than covered her two fingers with the past before finding a sharp stick that she thrust through the eyes of each Piranha. This both killed and kept each on the stick that she carried with her. When she was done she had eight fish to fill her belly with.

With no fire to cook Shelby ate three of the raw fish, each piece was taken with a savage bite as if she was killing each one over and over for the way her father died. For many weeks that was her diet as she found ways to survive in the deep jungle and her skill improved each day in catching small animal to eat.

Time pasted slowly and how long she sat starring at the big pool she didn't know. Shelby shook her head to tear away the memories of her young life as she leaned against the gate to the big house. She had found Mr. King was not on the grounds and could not understand how until she searched a quarter mile from the big house on the opposite side of the road leading to the big house and that was when she found the small cabin next to the stream. One canoe was still tied to the post but the seconds slip was empty. He had escaped in the night, either right before she began her operations or as she was fighting to get into the house. She had found a small trail leading to the tunnel at the base of the house that he must have used. But to do that, he had to have been ready to escape, he had to know someone was coming for him. And to know that, he had to have been tipped off, no one knew she was coming after him except one person, Director Gozares.

Chapter 20

Shelby stood still against a tree at the designated pickup point as the helicopter hovered overhead ready to throw down the long ladder. "Where the hell is she Captain, there's no one down there and we've been hovering for ten minutes, if she doesn't make it in the next five minutes we're leaving without her and if she's alive she can find her own way back."

"She's down their Director, she was there before we began hovering."

"Oh! Is that right Captain and I suppose she's right where we all can see her?"

"As a matter of fact Director you can."

"I can what captain, quit playing word games, where is she?"

"You see the three trees clustered in the very center of the pickup zone."

"I got eyes Captain, there pretty plain to see."

"Focus your eyes on the ground at the base of the middle tree."

"Ok, I got it, there's two big ferns growing from the base of the middle tree, so what."

"Check the small opening between the two ferns at the very base of the tree, what do you see?"

"Fern at the base of the tree----in the middle, hell Captain I don't see------Shit, how does she do that?

The camouflaged pant leg appeared in his vision and once that was in his focus he could trace the outline all the way up to her face. He involuntarily jerked his head back when he met her dark penetrating eyes looking directly at him, Captain Ruiz kicked the rope ladder out of the helicopter and it hung ten feet off the ground twenty feet from her.

Shelby looked at the message on her cell phone one more time before leaping to catch the ladder. It read, 'You are to be arrested and charged with disobeying a direct order not to proceed on your final mission. In addition you are to be charged with violating presidential order 231. The attempted assassination of a citizen of Colombia and the act which in itself is illegal, proceed at your own risk, I cannot help you.'

As the ladder ascends with Shelby attached at one end she notices the armed guard sitting next to the window she will be pulled through. As she made the last step and was pulled in Captain Ruiz only nodded as Shelby climbed around the soldier helping her aboard and sat next to him.

"Welcome aboard Agent Cruse." The Director said and smiled as she sat across from him and the guard that had his gun pointed squarely at her chest.

"You know what I've always liked about the Agency Cruse, it's the order of it, when an order is given and obeyed your always secure in the fact that you've done the right thing and no problems will come from higher ups."

Agent Shelby half snorted when the Director said that but she never took her eyes from him. If she were going to die, like maybe being pushed out of the helicopter, she would see it in his eyes before the order was given and he would be the first to die. For no man alive could stop the one blow she would deliver to his nose before the order was half out of his mouth. She waited and saw the hate in his eyes knowing the order was about to be given; she could even feel the tension in Captain Ruiz body. The threat would not come from him, instincts told her that the first threat would come from the soldier who had helped her up, as he had the look in his eyes that she had seen many times before when they knew that death would be coming from their actions.

She sensed more than felt the small movement of the soldier as his muscles tightened for the strike he was about to make. The shrill whistling of the two-way radio broke the tension as the operator spoke and than handed the set to Director Gozares. The Director acknowledges it was he and did nothing for the next several minutes but listen. Shelby watched as his facial expression hardens the more he listened, his only other word was that he understood before he handed the set back to the operator.

The Director leaned back and spoke to the pilot. "Change of plans, set a course for the presidential palace, twenty miles out radar will lock on and you will follow the beacon to the landing spot."

Shelby turned and pretended to look out the window as they made the turn from west to south but she made eye contact with Captain Ruiz and he gave only a slight raise of his eyebrows as if to say he knew nothing of this new direction.

Director Gozares, Captain Ruiz and Agent Shelby were escorted from the helicopter pad to the waiting black limousine and drove directly to the Presidential Palace. Not a word passed between the three as they disembarked the helicopter and rode the three miles to their destination. Once all three were secure in the outer office of the President and aid mentioned that the President would be here in ten minutes.

"I will do the talking, you two will speak only when spoken to and only when a direct question is directed towards you." The Director said, as he looked hard at both of them. Captain Ruiz only shrugged his shoulders; Agent Cruse starred the Director down until he broke eye contact. *I'll speak when ever I hell please* she as much said when looking at the Director.

The door opened and the Aide to the President motioned to Agent Cruse. "The president would like to talk to you Agent Cruse, Director, Captain Ruiz my assistant will escort you to the dinning room. The President will join you there as soon as the meeting with Agent Cruse is over." The Director opened his mouth to speak, thought better and walked out of the room behind the assistant along with Captain Ruiz who had a slight smile on his lips.

Agent Cruse was escorted into the presidential office where she found him standing beside a large oval wood desk. As the aide left the President extended his hand and with a wide grind shook hers firmly.

"It is a pleasure to meet you Agent Cruse, I have just finished reading your file and it is most interesting. This country is privileged to have such an accomplished Agent, and such a beautiful one at that. Please be seated," He motioned to a chair next to the one he was beginning to set in.

"I understand you failed the second part of your mission in the jungle around Mitu, I have to say Agent Cruse I'm please that you failed in your mission in the assassination of a citizen of Colombia. From the beginning of my Presidency I have worked with the leaders of our country to make our land a land of laws. Laws that can and will be enforced my all citizens of our great country."

"I never failed my mission Mr. President, someone informed the target that I was coming."

"Yes, I know Agent Cruse, I informed him."

"What! You're the one that let that son-of-a-bitch escape?"

"Yes Agent Cruse I---well actually I was not the one that informed him, one of Directors Gozares's agents contacted him on my behalf."

"Why! For God's sake Mr. President why would you let a man like that live?"

"You must have missed what I said earlier Agent Cruse, so I will repeat it for you! I have made it my number one priority to get the trust of the people of Colombia, that has been very hard because of previous governments and their complete disregards of the law. This country will be a country of laws that are obeyed, not just by the masses but for the elite and the powerful. We have a specific law that states no government or agency will approve any assassination against their own citizens. You ignored a Presidential Order but you also obeyed a direct order from the Director of your agency. You were put into a situation in which you could not win no matter what path you chose, therefore as of this moment your last assignment has been black boxed and it will stay sealed under National Security Laws for thirty years."

"Yes Agent Cruse I to wish Mr. King was not among the living but we have laws that can accomplish just such a scenario."

"Mr. President as much as I'm sure you won't believe me, I respect how you feel and I do believe in the laws of our country, I let my personal feelings cloud my judgment."

"That is what I have been told Agent Cruse, and it is the part of have decided to believe. You have a couple of true friends that have brought that to my attention. Now shall we get down to the reason I brought you here?"

"You never brought me here to punish me for the attempted assassination?"

"Of course not Agent Cruse, I wouldn't have needed to bring you here to punish you. You were stopped and the law was actually not broken because he was already gone when you attacked the compound."

"Why did Director Gozares inform him after he had given me the assignment, was it because you found out and intervened?"

"I'm sorry Agent Cruse, I have left you in the dark, let me fill in the spaces for you. Director Gozares did not inform Mr. King nor did he inform me about the order he had given you. Your friend informed me after he could not talk you out of the assignment."

"My friend? The only person other than Director Gozares that knew my assignment was Captain Ruiz and he was the one that tried to talk-------Captain Ruiz contacted you!"

"Yes Agent Cruse, Captain Ruiz was the one that informed me. And I must say if it wasn't for his persistence pestering of my Aide with text messages about every ten minutes I would never have found out about the secret operation."

"Than Director Gozares knows it was Captain Ruiz who told you about the operations, Mr. President Captain Ruiz has put himself in grave danger, you must do something to protect him."

"Oh I have already accomplished that Agent Cruse." The President reached over and pressed a button on his desk and spoke. "John would you please ask the Director to come in please."

As the door open and John walked through the President said to Agent Cruse.

"Agent Cruse let me introduce you to your new director, Director Ruiz." Director Ruiz gave a soft chuckle when he looked at Shelby, who had stood up and was completely in shock.

"I wish I had a camera to always have the look I'm seeing on your face Shelby. I do believe that is the first time in all our time together that I've found a look of surprise on your face."

Out of character, Shelby rushed over and gave the new Director a very hard hug before realizing what she had done and in embarrassment tried to apologize with a tongue that was tied in knots.

"No apology is necessary among friends Shelby, I'm just glad I was in time to help." Shelby saw the warm smile on the Presidents face as Director Ruiz spoke.

"Director Gozares has voluntary taken retirement and with my permission is now on his way out of our country. And now Agent Cruse let me explain why you are here. Another friend of yours, I must say you have some very influential friends in very high places, insisted you be part of this operation."

"Does the name Jordan Daniels ring a bell Agent Cruse?"

"Jordan Daniels! The F.B.I. Agent from the United States, yes sir he was one of my instructors at school."

"Director Ruiz has already been brought up to date on the operations but if I leave anything out or you feel something needs to be added step in at any time Director. Apparently Agent Cruse the text message you sent to Director Jordan Daniels stirred up one hell of a hornets nest in the United States. The United States is very hot to get their hands on Mr. King. It seems they have now found not only that he had two of their agents murdered but four of their informants also. Which scares them because that means someone has a mole in their mist. They want him bad and although most of the F.B.I. and other agents do not agree with you on what was being transported Agent Daniels want's you there to help to prove or disprove your theory. His exact words to our ambassador were; *you went in one direction while your team and the other three teams went in the opposite direction in solving a crime. When it was over you had the goods and they all came back with their tails between their legs and he wanted your skills pronto.*"

"Do they think Mr. King will be coming to the United States?"

"Yes they do. They feel he wants to confront his partners in the United States and take charge of finding all the drugs that are missing, or more likely stolen."

"I don't think Agent Cruse believes any of that, do you?" Watching Director Ruiz speak Shelby smiled and answered.

"No Sir Director, I don't. There is no reason for the transportation of drugs to take place like that; I don't know how many times I have to say it just doesn't make any since. But now, if it's drug money involved it makes perfect since. King wanted all the drug money collect, let's say in the last couple of years, to be able to laundry it. Where could you laundry that large amount of money, not in the United States, at lease not in one big swoop. But you could in a small island with secret banking laws that would than transfer the money to the Old Russian Republics."

"And two, King is not going to come to the United States, he's way to caucuses for that. His power base is in this country, now more than at any other time. Or at lease that's what he is thinking at this moment. He's safe somewhere in a nice cozy hideout bragging to himself and maybe anyone else around that the President of Colombia was the very one that tipped him off. And don't fool yourself Mr. President, in thinking he doesn't know who gave the ok to warn him. The drug cartels have very good listening post at the very highest places. He might not know why you did it but he knows for sure it was you."

"And that could help us in this case Agent Cruse, for he knows me only as 'Archaic', roughly translated it means, friend or person on the same side in a struggle. We can use that code to get to him when the time comes." Director Ruiz said as he studied Shelby's expression.

Chapter 21

Alex read the newspaper article once more before putting it down. Vera was watching to see what kind of reaction he would have when he finished reading the three-week-old paper. The report was about a man found dead in the Bethany cemetery at Rockwell and 63rd street. The report stated in looked like the man had been placed there a few days before with no identification. One of the policemen at the scene said it looked like he had a heart attack and might have been in the cemetery looking at a love ones head stone when it happened. He also said there were no signs of fowl play and the only concerned was he had no identification on him.

The second article Vera gave Alex to read was the short article of an abandoned moving van found in the parking lot of the Albertson store at Rockwell and 23rd street in Bethany. Once Alex and Vera came

149

back from Europe she scanned the daily Oklahoma beginning the day Alex ran into the man and the truck. When she spotted the articles she cut them out and waited until Alex came home and discussed it with him. Nothing else was found in the paper about the moving van once the Bethany police impounded it. But there was another article about the dead man found in the Bethany cemetery three weeks later. The article mentioned that the police still had not identified him and a picture was attached to the article of the man in the hopes someone would see and recognize him. The man writing the article mentioned that every human being needed to have a proper burial and not be put in the ground in a pauper plot.

The legal wheels were turning on purchasing the bank and keeping it a secret about who was doing the purchase. Vera was very good at seeing that all the legal documents were completed right and Alex thanked her a number of times for the help. After seeing what she did and the knowledge she had he knew for sure if he had not brought his wife in he would have totally messed it up. And the more he thought of it the more concern he became about what she had said at the beginning. And that was that people were right now looking for the money. They would have to keep a low profile he knew, and make sure no more of the money was spent. It would stay right here he had put it until they were ready to give it to the right law Enforcement agency. Vera at this point was not sure who that would be but most likely it would be the Drug Enforcement Agency.

Alex would lay in bed at night right before he went to sleep and he would dream about the two billion dollars boxed up and sitting in the U-Store buildings. What he could do with that money, he felt he could double the money every five to six years and he would go to sleep dividing the five and six by the amount of years he felt he would live. *Wow, he would always think, how could you even find things to invest that kind of money in?* But it seemed that just before he fell asleep his last thoughts were of the kind of people out there in the city or state looking for the money, which in turn caused some extreme nightmares.

Upon his wife's urging Alex reluctantly called his partner one more time to see if he would stop all of this nonsense and make things right for both of their families. Alex called the office first but was told he had not been there in more than a week, next he tried his house and a maid answered the phone. A maid! They had never required a maid before but all of a sudden they now had one. She told Alex he was at the Oklahoma City Country Club, and without any encouragement from Alex she explained that that was where they spent most of their time now.

Alex reached his partner dinning in the club with his wife; the conversation was very short. Chuck Witt, per his attorneys, was not to discuss anything about the company with either him or his wife and with that he hung up the phone. Later Alex was thankful of the calming influence his wife had on him for he was ready to go to the county club and throw a basket full of money in his partner's lap just to show him who really had the money.

"Don't get your blood pressure up Alex and quit trying to have a heart attack. You and I will have the ultimate satisfaction when we watch his face at the meeting when our attorney informs everyone that you and I own all the notes against the company, including the extra millions Chuck and you borrowed a few months ago."

Chapter 22

"Why did you do it Captain, excuse me! Director?" Shelby said as the helicopter lifted and headed for the International Airport in Bogota. "You are the one person I have put my complete trust in and yet you betrayed that trust by informing the President about the operations."

"Get one thing straight Agent Cruse, I am first and foremost a citizen of this country that I love very much, and unlike you I have been through and witnessed when the laws of the country meant nothing to the elite and the powerful. I have friends and even a few relatives that disappeared without a trace once the police picked them up when I was young. I will not try and compare, of what little I know what you must have went through as a child but nothing, and I mean nothing justifies exterminating another human being without the due process of law. Without the law we are nothing, not even as good as the men who flaunt the law before our faces and when we take it upon ourselves to break that law we are even below them."

"In the act of arresting someone or in the heat of battle we kill someone the moral societies of this world realizes we are doing our job as best as we can, including putting our own lives on the front line to protect there's. Why did I do it Shelby, because you know it was the right thing to do."

For a long time, sitting across from him, Shelby said nothing. Listening to his words in her mind while she starred out the window of the helicopter. Once in a while making eye contact for only an instance before looking away again. The pilot motioned ahead and announced they would be landing at the airport in Bogota in five minutes, at which time Shelby would catch a flight in fourteen minutes leaving for Washington D.C.

When the helicopter touched down one lone woman was standing with a briefcase under her arm waiting for Shelby to disembark. The helicopter and its occupants would be heading in another direction as soon as she stepped to the tarmac. Leaning over to step from the door Shelby turned to Director Ruiz who was quietly watching her.

"Thank you Captain," Shelby said, using the Title they both knew meant so much more to each of them. "Thank you for saving my soul" she said as she stepped from the helicopter but not before she saw one small tear escape from his eye which did not matched the flow that was fallen from her dark damp eyes as she strolled toward the waiting plane.

She had not felt such pain since the death of the old warrior as she walked away from the helicopter but at the same time a since of truth and comfort from a man she did not want to be away from. Why did it take one small incident for her to see the truth not only about herself but also about the man she was leaving behind? A small part of her heart had been penetrated that she thought could never again open up after the old warrior looked up at her with his dying eyes and pleaded for her to let him go.

Ten o'clock the next morning Agent Shelby was escorted from the receptionist desk at F.B.I. Headquarters down the polished marble hallway to the Assistant Directors Office of Jordan Daniels. Seven men and women were seated around a round oak table as she was shown in. Assistant Director Jordan Daniels stood and came forward as she entered the room.

"Agent Shelby Cruse it is an honor and a pleasure to meet you again, thank you for the e-mail."

"The same for me Director Daniels, it's been a long time, I knew the e-mail would stir things up but I never thought you would call me here."

"That it has but the memories are still very fresh of the night in Tulsa, Oklahoma when you made fools of four highly trained teams of students that were to be graduating in four weeks."

As they spoke every man and woman in the room was sizing up the Agent from Colombia that the academy still talked about. Most believed that with each passing year her exploits at the academy became bigger and bigger. Only the ones that cared to read her complete file was in awe of her skills. The rest would soon discover what the few knew.

For three hours the group discussed the case, each agent detailing what they knew and what they could guess was happening. When they finished Agent Cruse went through the information she had gathered and also speculated to what she thought had happened and were going to happen.

Agent Hoffman seemed to speak for the group, Shelby noticed, when something was discussed that went in the opposite direction that she seemed to be taking.

"I don't get where your coming from Agent Cruse, you have told us nothing that would shed light on why you think the merchandise was money. To me it points to drugs just as it always has, please remember we have been following this man and his operations in the United States for more than ten years and not once have we found large amounts of money. On the other hand we have intercepted a number of large shipments of drugs into the United States that can be traced directly back to his organization."

"Agent Hoffman, in your dealings with other drug lords and distributors have you found large amounts of money along with the drugs?"

"Yes we have."

"Have you ever found large amounts of money when you intercepted shipments of drugs from Mr. King?"

"No, we have not, in fact I don't believe we have found any cash."

"Isn't that strange you found cash in every bust but never from his shipments or arrests of his men? Mr. King has had forty years of experience in hiding his money. He controls a number of companies in Colombia, that's how he laundries his money in our country. Nowhere have I found that he owns or is part owner of any company in the United States; I think he's afraid of the controls you have in your country. It's very hard to laundry a large amount of cash when the Fed.'s are looking at every transaction above nine thousand nine hundred and ninety-nine dollars."

"But, if he could get his money out of the United States, say into offshore banks or even across the ocean than the money trail would be much harder to find. I believe Mr. King has been planning this for a couple of years, in Colombia his power base are about as big as he can go. Bringing money back into Colombia would do him no good and as I said I believe he's afraid he will lose his money if he tries to laundry it in your country."

"You talk about him being so sharp Agent Cruse, how is it he lost the truck load of money if that's what it was?"

"I don't think he lost it Agent Hoffman."

"Uh, would you care to explain that to us Agent Cruse." Director Daniels said, looking surprised as the rest of the men and women in the conference.

"I think he had the truck stolen, I think he double crossed his partners in the United States."

"And what great insight do you have to believe that?" One of the women agents said a lot more sweetly than she meant.

Calmly looking at the agent whom had spoken Agent Cruse smiled slightly and said. "Because of the two men who were driving the missing truck."

That stunned every agent in the room including Director Daniels because every agent knew they had not given a second thought to who was driving the truck other than they were the ones Mr. King insisted would be the final drivers. Director Daniels rocked back and forth in his chair and nodded his head as he looked out into space before finally speaking.

"And you are going to tell us,"-----Director Daniels stopped and thumbed through his report, finally stopping on the sixth page. "Who Doug Ringo and Hernando Kling are?" Shelby smiled as she made eye contact with each agent in the room almost as if saying, *'Do your homework folks.'*

"Doug Ringo is second in command of his whole operations, has been for more than twenty years." The room erupted with every one talking at once until Director Daniels raised his hand and pointed to Agent Hoffman to speak.

"Agent Cruse, I suppose you can be excused because you live and work in Colombia, but we know who the second in command is in Mr. Kings operations, it's Jose Manual. He's lived here in the United States for approximately fifteen years; he's a citizen of Panama. For the last ten years he has flown to Colombia once a year to meet with Mr. King to get the orders were sure Mr. King does not want spoken over the phone." Every head in the room was shaking in agreement with what Agent Hoffman was saying except Director Daniels. Director Daniels only listened and watched the expression on Agent Cruse's face.

Shelby again made eye contact with every agent in the room before speaking again. "Jose Manual actually made three trips to Colombia each year for the last eleven years. Once each year he would fly from the United States to Colombia under his own name and be met by Mr. King. The other two times he drove to Mexico City and boarded a plane using the name of Pat Boehm. These two flights landed in Panama City where he was driven to Torg International Investment Company, exactly twenty-four hours later he would be driven into Colombia to meet in secret with Mr. King. After the meeting he would be driven back to Panama

City where he caught a plane to Mexico City." Again the room erupted as each agent tried to say something to her and again Director Daniels raised his hand for quite before nodding to Agent Hoffman to speak.

"Torg International Investment Company is one of the largest companies in the world. They have their fingers in every international agreement that comes down the pike and the United Nations banking branch uses them almost exclusively. We have been trying for years to get someone inside either place but have been blocked at every turn. What would Jose Manual have to do with Torg?"

"Who owns Torg International Mr. Hoffman?"

"We don't know, our accounting branch has been trying to untangle the agreements that cross almost all borders on three continents. We have the figureheads down, but not who really runs the company, not who the real power behind it is."

"And now you're going to tell us we now know who the power behind Torg is Agent Cruse?" Said Director Daniels.

"Jose Manual started the company from his drug smuggling business more than forty years ago. He layered company after company underneath the company until now all you see is Torg International. It would take the right codes and the right people to unravel the companies and get to him. He's not Mr. Kings second in command, they worked together as mules in their youths before branching out on their own. He's Mr.

King's secret partner in the United States; they both wanted it to look like he was just a worker. It worked very well too, for years now your agency never had a clue he was flying out of Mexico City to do the real work he was the most interested in." At first the group was too stunned to say much before everyone in the room began to speak to her at once.

Shelby leaned back in her chair and waited as the agents tried to argue with her, Director Daniels and finally with each other until for the third time Director Daniels raised his hand for quite.

"Your still haven't answered the question Agent Cruse, who are the two drivers?" Director Daniels said as he smiled at her. Shelby liked the Director, he was still the sharpest one in the room, never letting a detail slip away when other things tried to set it aside or make you forget you had it on your mind and everyone else realized they should have asked that very same question.

"Doug Ringo, as I said was his second in command, was always going to be from the day he was born. Doug Ringo is his son and to find out early what his own flesh and blood was made of he ordered his son to execute a man on his sixteenth birthday. The man was his mother's brother, his uncle." Most in the room were shaking their heads back and forth trying to swallow this new information that was beginning to make them look like fools.

"The only other man he trusted that much was his number one body guard, and that's who was the second man in the truck, Hernando Kling. That truck was not stolen ladies and gentlemen, it was driven by two men that had orders to take it to, I believe, Tulsa, Oklahoma. From there it was to be loaded on a yacht Mr. King owned and than sailed out to sea to some unknown destination." Shelby let that sink in before putting in the small jab she felt was necessary to the men and woman in the room.

"It's understandable you would know nothing about his early days since you work in the United States and had very little dealing with the drug trade in Colombia at that earlier time." Director Daniels rose quickly when she made her point and said a few remarks before dismissing the agents.

"Let's have a bite to eat Agent Cruse and you can fill me in on anything else you think we have missed. You know Shelby you will be required to work with some of the men and women at the meeting wouldn't it be better not to get on the wrong side of them?"

"Wrong side of them! Director let me set you straight on something up front. The President of my country ordered me to come to the United States and assist you, and your team, in any way I can and that I will do as best as I can. But I don't play politics and I don't respect incompetence in any agent."

"Tell me something I don't already know Agent Cruse, if you recall I was your teacher in a number of your classes at the academy."

"Sorry Director Daniels, that was uncalled for, I apologize, you know I have very high respect for you and your agency and I couldn't have had a better mentor while training in your country.

Chapter 23

The F.B.I. set up a special team to work with Agent Cruse, their office was located on the outskirts of Houston, Texas as that was the approximate location of the last sighting of the missing truck, or at lease where Jose Manual said the truck was last seen. Shelby had flown into Tulsa, Oklahoma with Agent Huffman and was in the process of renting a car when Director Daniels called and said they had made an identification of a man found in the Cache river three weeks ago. The man was identified through dental records as Doug Ringo. After looking over her Oklahoma map Shelby decided to travel to the scene in her vehicle. It would be straight down Turner Turnpike to Oklahoma City, connecting with the H.E. Bailey Turnpike to the small town of Geronimo a few miles south of Lawton. Putting the red light on top of the roof on the driver side Shelby floored the gas pedal and drove the vehicle over a hundred miles an hour down the road. Agent Hoffman contacted the Oklahoma Highway Patrol and informed them of their situation and that they were in a hurry.

Traveling on any Oklahoma Turnpike you have to stop in a number of places to pay the toll unless you have the electronic pass attached to your windshield, in which case you could speed straight through the toll lane designated for such a pass. Knowing the agent's car did not have a Pike Pass the Highway Patrol called the turnpike authority.

"This is Sergeant Nolls of the Highway Patrol, please connect me with the Director of Tolls." After two different turnpike employees put Sergeant Nolls on hold the connection was made to the proper employee.

"This is Randy Moore, Director of Tolls, how may I assist you Sergeant Nolls?"

"Director Moore I have an F.B.I. vehicle, License plate number SXY-239, with it's red light on coming down Turner Turnpike and will be connecting to H.E. Bailey Turnpike, please notify the proper people in your department about the situation and do not try and stop."

"I am imputing the information in our computers now Sergeant Nolls give me a few more seconds to make sure the information has been received by our toll. Ok Sergeant the vehicle has full clearance, god speed and good luck."

Shelby and Agent Hoffman reached the small town of Geronimo in two hours and forty minutes. Director Daniels was waiting when they drove up.

"Agent Cruse, Hoffman get in my car and well drive to Cache River, it's only a few miles away. The body was found almost a month ago Agent Cruse and it had been in the water for sometime. The only reason we became involved in the first place was the way the man was found. His body was strapped to one of those dollies you find in moving vans. Of course he had a small bullet hole in the back of his head, but the dolly was heavy enough to sink him to the bottom of the river. They had a large rain a day before a fisherman found him, must have washed him up from the bottom, either that or he got lighter when the fish ate most of his flesh and he floated to the top."

"When did you make the identification, Director Daniels?"

Director Daniels looked up at Shelby and was about to say something before he changed his mind and said something else. "The call came to me an hour before I called you Agent Cruse." The tone in his voice let her know he did not like her line of questioning, insinuating that he might have known a long time before he called her.

"Who found him?"

"Some young man, out fishing before dawn for a few hours before he headed for his job. I have his name in the file if you need it."

"Thanks, maybe later, you said he was secured to a dolly! Did it have a name on the dolly of the trucking company?"

"No."

"So the men were in a big truck, which was as I expected, was it maybe a household moving van. One of those massive trucks that could carry a lot of cargo."

"I don't see why you would think it was a moving van any more than any other large truck, like for instance a Rider Truck."

"Could be Director, I was just throwing out words, sometimes when you do that a word will catch something in the wind."

"Tell us what this does to Mr. Kings plans?"

"I don't know Director, but it means he has a big problem, now not only his partners lose their money but he lost the money he stole from them. Maybe they took it back from him but if they did it would surprise me. The man still with the truck was a very loyal person to King. A very cruel person but loyal for many years."

"Where are you going to start Shelby?"

"I'm going back to Tulsa, try and find that boat and see where it leads me. Care to tag along Director?"

"I was just going to suggest that very thing Agent Cruse. Agent Hoffman you come along with us, I'm going to need you to do some research on the computer."

"That reminds me Director, you said you would give me a laptop with complete security clearance, have you started on that yet?"

"Already done Cruse, it's in the back of my car, drive over there Hoffman and I'll get the lap top for Agent Cruse." All the way back on the drive to Tulsa Shelby was quietly entering information in her laptop. One of the things she asked information about was anything out of the usual from the police departments in Oklahoma and Texas. There were thousands of hits that she then fed into a program that tried to connect any dots that might be connected to the case.

Just as they were entering Tulsa Shelby's computer began to flash a green arrow indicating one of her bits of information had made a hit. The Catoosa Port Authorities had filed a notice with their home office in Washington D.C. requesting permission to evict a yacht that was now one month beyond their authorized docking permit. Leaning over towards Director Daniels Shelby turned her laptop towards him and said.

"Care to wager a guess who owns this yacht." Director Daniels shot up fast and typed in a few strokes after reading the report. In thirty seconds the number of the yacht came back.

"Bingo, it's your Mr. Kings yacht, good work Agent Cruse, Hoffman drive on to Catoosa."

Chapter 24

It was after ten at night when the three of them drove to a parking lot a few blocks from where the yacht was moored. After calling for a backup team the three started for the docking in almost total darkness. There were no streetlights in the area and only one lone light at the end of the dock, at the other end of where the yacht was docked. They studied the yacht for half an hour without seeing any kind of movement on the deck or in the wheelhouse.

"Listen up Hoffman and Cruse, there's the one gang plank in the middle of the ship and a ladder that is still hanging over the back of the ship. Hoffman you take the plank, I'll climb the ladder. Give me time to clear the deck before you start up the gangplank, Cruse you say here until you see us both on the deck of the ship and then come on up." Shelby's eyes turned black and cold but before she could say anything Director Daniels shut her up.

"Agent Cruse you are here at the request of my government to help and you have been assigned to me, therefore you will obey my orders. Are you going to have a problem with that order?"

Seething with anger, her black eyes shooting darts at Director Daniels, Shelby eased down to a squat before speaking. "No Sir!" Only her deep respect for Director Daniels made her stay where she was instead of hauling ass for the gangplank. "Kind of ironic don't you think Director, here we are back in the same area we visited years ago on my last training mission with the F.B.I.?"

"I guess that means you have come full circle Agent Cruse. I suppose next you will be asking if you can join our team." The Director and Agent Hoffman watched as Shelby's smile took up most of her lower face and both men's' heart skipped a beat at the beauty they saw in her smile. Shelby slowly shook her head back and forth before the smile faded and than they watched as she pealed out of her clothes. When she was done both men stood looking at her with open mouths as she wore only a thin skintight one piece black leotard that hid nothing. Embarrassed with what they were thinking both men turned back toward the ship. Shelby flashed a mouth full of white teeth as they turned their backs on her.

Both agents waited in the darkness until they saw that the Director had climbed the last step of the ladder and was disappearing over the side onto the ship. As Agent Hoffman started forward Shelby touched his elbow and spoke.

"I saw movement by the wheelhouse going around to the port side, stay here until we can find out where he is."

"How the hell could you see anything, it's pitch black on the ship, must have been the shadow of a cloud or something else."

"Stay where you are Agent Hoffman, you start up that gangplank and you're a sitting duck!"

"Like the Director said, Agent Cruse, stay here until you see us both on the ship." Drawing his gun Agent Huffman confidently stepped out of the shadows and headed for the gangplank. Shelby shook her head as she scanned the deck to see if she could make out where the man was hiding. He was there she knew, waiting for him to start up the gangplank. Raising the gun she began to scan the area in front of him, at the same time darting a look to the stern of the ship to see if Director Daniels was coming forward.

As Agent Huffman reached the middle of the gangplank Shelby spotted the Director, moving in a slow circle away from the gangplank. He knows where the man is Shelby thought, she could tell by his posture and the movement right before a kill was to begin. Shifting her sights again towards the middle of the ship she spotted him, or rather the barrel of the gun coming out of the darkness and swinging towards Agent Hoffman. Hoffman was now only three steps from the top of the gangplank, his head and shoulders exposed.

Shelby swung her gun towards the barrel sticking out of the darkness at the same time she let out a blood curling sound, a sound that's made when an animal has attacked another animal and it knows its own death is only a split second away. It froze all three men in place for one startling moment before the gun sticking out of the shadows spit out two silent bullets that struck Agent Hoffman in his left armpit right below the body armor he was wearing. Agent Hoffman was thrown off the gangplank and landed some twenty feet below, his body on the dock and his head hanging over looking down into the blackness of the water.

Shelby saw that he did not move and thought for sure he was dead. And he would have been if not for the death scream that made him turn his body away from the bullets that were heading for his head. He was in critical condition but would live if they could get him to medical care quickly. As she watched him fall she saw from the corner of her eye the flash of the gun a second time, but this time it was aiming in the area Director Daniels was in.

Shelby knew the Director had been hit, you never forget the sound a bullet makes as it enters a human body, she also heard his grunt as the impact of the bullet pushed all the air from his lungs. What Shelby did not know was that the body armor he wore stopped the bullet from doing any other damage. But the impact threw his body backwards and his head hit a metal post knocking him out. He had almost succeeded in getting behind the man on the ship but had to expose himself when he climbed from the deck to the wheelhouse and that's when the bullet struck him.

In less than a second the man had kicked his gun away and in the same swift movement looped a rope around his hand before pulling the rope tight and bringing Daniels hands behind his back. Next he looped the rope around his chest and neck before putting it through the secondary eye of the anchor box and pulled tight. When Director Daniels came to a few seconds later he was hogged tied and every time he tried to move his breathing was cut off. The man knew his way around a ship and he was big. Director Daniels knew the man was the Jack Strong mentioned on the phone. He had been sent a picture and update of the man and he knew he was a dangerous opponent.

The man was six feet four and all muscle and he was a karate expert who had his own club years ago before getting in trouble with the law. He also was picked up for murder but the authorities could not make the charges stick. He walked from the Tulsa jail laughing at the guards.

Director Daniels couldn't see the man but he could see out over the dock and the gangplank. He also knew there was no way the bullets could have missed Agent Hoffman, besides the sound of his body hitting the deck was enough to let him know he had not landed on his feet. Peering into the darkness at the edge of the pier he tried to find Agent Cruse but after three sweeps he gave up. There had also been no movement from Jack Strong any time after Director Daniels opened his eyes. He had no clue where he was but he strained his ears to try and hear something.

Where is Agent Cruse, he thought to himself, *is she helping Hoffman? And what was that God-awful animal sound that came just before Strong fired at Hoffman?* Sweeping his eyes back and forth to where he knew Shelby should be he found nothing but blackness, no movement, no shadows, nothing but------wait! Out of the corner of his eye he spotted a small movement at the spot he knew she should be. Moving his eyes to either side of the spot he tried again to find what had caught his eye before. The eyes played tricks when looking directly at something in the dark and he learned to focus just a shade away from where he needed to look and that's when he saw the dark outline of her.

As he tried to maintain his focus on the dark figure Daniels wondered what she was going to do, he knew she had witnessed Hoffman getting shot and he felt good that she had obeyed his command not to do anything until she saw both of them on the deck. Now he knew she was safe and soon the backup team would be here to help.

He smiled as he thought of her seething in fury as she obeyed his orders, at lease she never tried some crazy action to get on the ship. If she had she surely would have been killed just like Hoffman but she used her sen--------Director Daniels never got to finish his thought as a blur raced from the darkness. She was heading straight for the gangplank at a speed he could not believe. His mouth dropped open as he watched the blur reach the first step of the gangplank. *No Shelby*, Daniels thought, *you will never make it*. Desperately he twisted his head around as much as he could to try and locate Jack Strong but no movement or noise came from any direction on the ship. Daniels wanted to shout at Shelby to stop, turn around and wait but he knew that in a few seconds either she or Jack Strong would be dead.

Daniels had spent less than a second looking for Jack Strong before returning his focus to Shelby and to his amazement she was already halfway up the gangplank. That's when he saw the silver barrel emerge from the shadows and began to level. Turning back to Shelby he saw she was now two thirds of the way up the gangplank, but it was to late, the gun was level and she had no body armor. Director Daniels opened his mouth to shout words that he knew would do no good as Strong squeezed the trigger on his automatic.

Shelby leaped, not for the top of the gangplank, but at an angle that would take her four feet to the left of the top step. She felt the ball of her left foot touch the railing at the same instance she focused her strength on the large muscle in that leg. Without stopping any of her forward motion she propelled her body fifteen feet onto the deck of the ship. As her foot landed on the deck Shelby rolled and disappeared into the darkness.

If Director Daniels mouth had not been attached he would have been trying to pick it up off of the deck. That leap was impossible! She was at lease twenty feet from the top when she leaped and she leaped upwards! Hell an Olympic long jump champion would have been lucky to jump that far and he would have been jumping on level ground! What amazed him even more was the way her body turned and twisted; it looked more like an animal's movement rather than humans.

Silence, Director Daniels heard only his own breathing, which was labored because of the tightness of the rope around his neck and chest. *Where were they?* The only light on this side of the ship was smack in the middle, you could see clear a twenty-foot square before the light faded from semi-darkness to complete blackness. Daniels mind raced back to the moment Shelby leaped, he heard and saw the flash of the gun at the same instance as she began her leap, but from her movements at the top of the rail it did not appear as if she was hit. But how could he have missed her, he was no more than thirty feet away and with a clear view for his shots.

The Director also knew he had not heard the familiar sound of bullets hitting flesh, so he was sure she had not been hit. Maybe her being all black and running so damn fast surprised him enough that he never compensated enough for how fast she was. He still couldn't believe she did it and he knew there was not an agent under his command that could have done what she just did. Now, where the hell is she and where is Strong?

Shelby crouched low, moving one foot or hand at a time never putting one or the other down until she felt nothing but deck. She could see Director Daniels tied securely by the anchor rope, she had watched for a few seconds to make sure he was able to breath and she saw that he could if he would only quit trying to struggle. Jack Strong she knew was in the darkest part of the deck with his back against the wheelhouse and she was some thirty feet to his left. Getting to the position she knew was the best angle for her attack she slowly lowered her body to a squatting stance and waited. She was good at waiting, the old warrior had taught her well on that subject. '*Wait out your enemy, time is always on your side. Most humans and animals become impatient with the passage of time, wait for that and than strike when they're impatience makes them weak. Remember the two laws, surprise and death; strike with surprise for that will not allow the enemy to group all his forces. And the first violent attack should cause death for if you do not secure death that will be your most dangerous time for the enemy will turn on you without thinking and use only instincts, which is unpredictable.*

Chapter 25

Jack Strong pressed his back against the wall knowing he was protected from the rear. His heart was still racing hard from the episode of a few seconds ago. He had her in his sights and yet the bullets missed, how someone could jump that far going up hill was remarkable but even more amazing was the speed as she raced from the darkness and up the gangplank. He had watched as two men came out of the darkness less than ten minutes ago and tried to board his vessel. One he killed easily and the other was now tied up good and tight, he would extract the information he needed from that one when he was finished with her.

She had not surprised him when he saw her running from the darkness, for he had kept his eyes on that very spot, he figured there was at lease one backup, maybe even two. The movements of her legs as she raced up the gangplank disturbed him, he felt like he was watching something other than just human take the steps three at a time in full stride. All runners needed to focus their eyes on the steps when running either up hill or down hill when going that fast but her eyes were directed always upward towards the railing. It was as if her feet and legs were disconnected from the rest of her body and had only one function, to float above anything they could touch.

Jack Strong also noticed something else too; he had been waiting on this ship way to long, leaving only to re supply foodstuff. He had not been with a woman for weeks and when she ran towards the gangplank with her arms pumping up and down he watched her breast keep pace with each arm. There were no implants in that lady, he could tell that for sure. And there was nothing left for his imagination with the outfit she was wearing, but it also pissed him off because it was hard to track her with the night being so black and she wore nothing but black, which made it even harder.

He had lost her when she did her barrel roll and now it was going on four or five minutes, why no sound from her? Where is she? Did she get hurt on the roll or did one of my bullets find its mark? All these things kept going around Jacks mind as he kept his back pressed firmly against the wood.

Five more minutes past with the only sound being the Directors hard breathing or his coughing when he struggled to much and his air would get cut off until he came back to the one position he could lay in without it happening.

Shelby could feel the tension building; could almost feel the heat coming from Jack Strong and she could smell the sweat beginning to slide down his back. Soon, soon he will make a move and my strike will come. *Think good thoughts Mr. Jack Strong for they are about to be your last and I will have eliminated another piece of scum from the human population. How many have I eliminated, how many have I stopped from destroying another family? But they keep on coming no matter what I do, they will never stop until the smart minds of this world wakes up and realizes they have taken the wrong road to stop all of this. Why are people so damn blind?*

Shelby felt it before her eyes saw the small movement moving away from the wall of the wheelhouse, he was moving, standing almost straight up with his gun hand half extended from his body. He was moving away from her which made it almost to easy as she sprung from the darkness and was on top of him before even the Director knew she was there.

Shelby's first strike, with her left hand, was to the base of his skull at the fleshly part of the spine as her right hand streaked toward his windpipe. To her shock neither blow connected its target. Her left hand made contact with something soft that also absorbed the power of her thrust and the right hand made contact with the gun Jack Strong had pulled back the second before she struck. The gun went flying from his hand

and the movement sent both of them into the small circle of light. Now Shelby could see why her first strike to his spine was ineffective, he was wearing some kind of thick collar. Jack Strong had been plagued with neck pain for many years and when he had time to sit he would always put on the heated collar that was filled with sand to sooth the pain.

Shelby landed on her back as Jack was spun in her direction and as he made his turn he kicked out with his left leg and caught her on her left buttock lifting her two feet off the deck. The blow was mild because Shelby had seen it coming and had turned and gone with the power of his kick.

Both attacked at the same time, Shelby blocking three straight blows to her body and Jack blocking two blows to his head. Director Daniels watched the scene go to slow motion as each thrust and blocked blow after blow from the other. He was so much larger than she was and Jordan knew that if Jack could get one good strike to her body she might not be able to take it. And he had no more thought it when Jack faked a thrust which she blocked but she could not bring her body around to stop the real one from coming. It landed on her left ear and sent her sprawling on the deck, as she leaped to her feet he was already standing over her and he reached down and grabbed her crouch, lifting her eyes to his level as he grinned and squeezed.

That was his mistake for he had only one hand to ward off her blows, and he only blocked two of the four that found their mark on the side of his windpipe and on the bridge of his nose. Letting go of her crouch he threw a glancing blow to the side of her left eye and another blow that she flocked. The force of the block and her gong with the force of the blow caused her to be thrown to the corner of the light while he stumbled to the middle. To Director Daniels it felt like he was watching a fight in a ring with lights shinning down on the two fighters. He could see blood dripping from Jack Strong's nose and Shelby's left eye was swelling fast, in another few minutes it would be completely closed.

Shelby stood in a half crouch as Daniels watched her whole body began to relax, it was as if someone had turned the light off inside of her and her muscles became smaller. Jack Strong saw it too, standing ten feet away from her but he was smart enough to know she was still dangerous. Instead of moving toward her he spotted the gun laying on a wooden box five feet to his right. When he looked at the gun so did Shelby and Daniels watched the transformation start. Jack did not, he was to intent on wanting to get the gun and blow her head off, the hell with capturing her and doing what he wanted with her, now he just wanted her dead.

Five small steps would bring him to the gun and she was ten feet away, the advantage was his, he thought. As he took his first step sideways, always keeping his eyes on her, both he and Daniels saw the muscles began to ripple in her legs. Daniels thought it looked almost like small waves washing up on the beach, one after the other the muscles would start in her lower legs and progress upwards. Daniels would swear later than each time the wave reached her thighs the muscles would get bigger. On his second step towards the gun Shelby's left arm raised until her hand was even with her shoulder and her right arm extended half cocked at eye level.

Director Daniels focused his sight on her left hand that rested next to her shoulder and he blinked twice to make sure he saw what was happening. Shelby's left hand began to fold until the hand no longer resembled a true hand but became one solid form that looked like a blunt spear with a very small point at the end. The right hand was balled into a fist with only the middle knuckle exposed. She never took her eyes from Jacks as he made his third step towards his goal.

Daniels was screaming in his head for Shelby to attack before he reached the gun, you can't outrun a bullet nor can you swat it away for Christ sake. *Don't wait until its too late Shelby!* These things he said in his mind but his eyes were glued to her.

Jack took his fourth and fifth step and was standing right above the weapon but had not yet taken his eyes away from Shelby. It was frightening to him to watch her, so calm and cool, *what can she possibly do to stop me? Why is she just standing there? I've never fought such a fighter,* how could she be so strong, she had hurt him and hurt him bad, worse than any other fight he had ever been in. Jack couldn't believe a woman could be that good, she was better than any man he had ever fought and he knew she had the capabilities, just as he did, to kill with one strike. He was not going to get any closer to her, he would put a couple of bullets in her pretty breast and dump her downstream with the alligators.

For a full ten seconds the two locked eyes before Jack Strong looked down to see exactly where the gun was. Director Daniels saw her eyes narrow, almost like a cat that was getting ready to pounce when Jack looked down at the gun.

Director Daniels watched as Jack bent down and began to reach for the gun and that was when she moved. Before his hand was half way to the gun she was five feet from him and when his hand touched the gun her left hand tore through his chest just below the breastbone while her right knuckle crushed his windpipe. His fingers never had time to curl around the weapon before he began falling backwards. He was dead before he hit the deck, his crushed windpipe would have killed him quickly but he was already dead when the blow struck his windpipe. The first blow, Shelby's left hand, penetrated the chest cavity with such force that it ripped his heart from the two main arteries.

Director Daniels still could not believe what he had just witnessed. She was in one place and the next half- second she was on top of Jack Strong throwing two killing blows. No one could move that fast, no one! And the penetration through the chest wall, the force it required to do that took inhuman strength. He lay still as he watched her ripe part of Jacks shirt off to wipe the blood from her hand before calmly walking over and kneeling beside him.

"You scared me Jordan Daniels, I thought for sure you were going to chock yourself to death before I could help you." This she said in a calm soft voice and a smile that lit up her face as if she was helping some small boy bandage his scraped knee. *She's a freak, a Goddamn freak*! Jordan thinks as she begins to until the rope. When she had untied the last of the rope and helped him up Jordan had the overwhelming urge to run, run as fast and as far away from her as he could. Jesus! He thought, what am I thinking, she just saved my life, get a hold of your self Daniels, for Christ sake get a hold of yourself! Shelby walked toward the gangplank with Jordan following behind looking her body over from head to foot. There was nothing hidden from his view as he took in the power of her legs and the slight swing side to side of her hips. Power and strength radiated from every pore of her body. I wonder what she would do, he thought, if I reached out and pinched her on the cheek of her butt. Then he smiled inward, God I wouldn't do that for all the money in the world, for one I'd never have the chance to spend it, unless she decided to only cripple instead of killing me.

Chapter 26

Shelby put her foot on the gangplank before turning towards Jordan as he looked into the smoldering blackness deep in her eyes.

"Did you have enough time to examine me Director or would you like me to stand here facing you so you can complete your examination?"

Startled Jordan tried to mutter something funny but the words came out in a jumble that made no since at all. His eyes locked on hers, he tried to think of something to say and finally shrugged his shoulders and said. "Sorry about that."

"I like that about you Jordan Daniels, you're honest, sorry if I embarrassed you." Shelby than raced down the gangplank to where Agent Hoffman was lying, leaving Jordan to shake his head. *How does she do that! Did I breathe hard or make some kind of sound? Like I thought a few seconds ago, she's a freak of nature!*

As Director Daniels walked down the gangplank the backup team arrived and helped Shelby stabilize Agent Hoffman before taking him to the Tulsa Regional Hospital. Agent Hoffman's life was saved but he would never work as an agent again, he lost the use of his left arm and one lung.

The next morning relaxing in the back seat of the vehicle with Director Daniels he watched her as she put on the last bit of makeup to try and cover most of the black and purple around her eye. No matter what she put on that eye he knew she would not be able to cover up the shiner. She could still see out of the eye but just barely.

Shelby was deep in thought as their driver headed out of Tulsa, Oklahoma towards Dallas. Both had decided Dallas was the place to set up a command post and work up and down the corridor of I-35 and I-45.

"I've known you for a long time Agent Cruse, worked closely with you on a number of training exercise and I've seen how good you are. That's why I tried to get you to stay in the United States and become an F.B.I. Agent. Your actions last night are going to make a very hard report even harder to make since to anyone reading it. I haven't a clue how you accomplished some of the things you did last night but the Agency and I am grateful. But I am also personally concerned for you, even though, as I said, I have known you for a long time, I don't know you at all. You keep everything inside, Hell Shelby I don't even know if you like ice cream! Isn't that a crazy thing to say, but what I'm getting at is, I'm your friend and I have broad shoulders if you ever need to use them. Like the saying from a book that I read a long time ago, 'No one is an island into himself."

"I read the book Director." Shelby said as she leaned back in the seat and closed her eyes.

"All I meant Shelby was that everyone needs someone else once in a while?"

"I know what you meant Director." They road in silence for minutes before the Director spoke.

"How did you do that?"

"What?" Shelby said as she opened her eyes and looked at him.

"How did you do what you did with your hand." He said as he touched her left hand. Sighing Shelby looked down at her hand and her eyes drifted away for a second before she replied.

"The old warrior taught me."

"That's what I mean Shelby, you talk in circles but never give any information. This must be the fifth or sixth time I have hear you say the old warrior taught you or showed you when I asked you something."

Turning sideways in the seat Shelby reached over and put his hand on her left hand before putting her right hand on top of his.

"Feel the movement of my joints?" she said as she formed her hand into the dull spear he had seen the night before, the form that went through Jack Strong's chest like a surgeons knife.

"I can't do that with my hand, can't even begin to try!"

"Neither did I the first few thousand times he made me try."

"Who was this person Shelby? Where were you raised?"

Looking at Director Daniels and than at the agent driving the vehicle Shelby hesitated in what if any thing she wanted or should tell the Director. When Daniels saw her look at the driver he mistook what she was thinking; he reached between the seats and pushed the button that raised the petition between the driver and the passengers in the back.

"So you want to know the why about me Director? Why am I here? Why am I doing the things I do? Why my personnel life is not a public record? Why I can do some of the things you think are impossible? Nothing is impossible Director, not if we put our full mind to the task, modern man has forgotten to use the DNA that's stored in each of us and has been from the beginning." With an almost small child like smile and sad eyes Shelby leaned close to Jordan Daniels and said.

"So you want to know what makes me tick Jordan Daniels?"

Chapter 27

Shelby leaned back in the seat, closed her eyes and was quiet for sometime before she spoke. Shelby told about her childhood, about the big house on the hill that housed Hector King. Of the pretty white dress and the terror of the big house and the fleeing before coming back to find her mother dead and the man who killed her mother and tried to rape her. She told of the flight back into the jungle and living on Piranha and anything that crawled.

"For two months Jordan I lived in the jungle alone, fighting for survival from the snakes and big cats that wanted to make a meal of me or kill me with one strike from their fangs. I don't know how I survived those two months; I was barely nine years old. In the middle of my third month I was a skinny naked little girl. My clothing had rotted away and the only tool I had was the sharp stick I would carve to catch fish with and to fend off the animals. You would be amazed at the sounds and smells you acquire when you're all alone, afraid the next tree or bush will hold something that could kill or eat you. But I was to young, I never had the necessary skills to survive, I had been lucky up to that point but I was becoming weaker and weaker. One day I smelled smoke, I couldn't tell where it was coming from or see it but I smelled it. I began walking against the wind hopping the wind was blowing the smell towards me. For two days I walked, stopping only to drink and hunt for something to eat. There were no streams I crossed in those two days so all the food I found was insects." Director Daniels kept his mouth shut and his ears open as he listened to the amazing tale this beautiful woman beside him was telling. His heart went out like never before to the small child as he saw in his mind the struggle and danger she endured as she made her way through a sometimes almost impenetrable jungle. Could he have survived that long, not likely even as an adult?

"The end of the second day I stopped smelling smoke and that's when I gave up the will to live. I curled up in a ball at the base of a large tree and waited to die, whether from snakebite or one of the big cats, I never cared. I couldn't have defended myself anyway because I felt like I was too weak to even walk. The next thing I remember the sun was shinning through the tops of the trees and a snake, an anaconda I thought was wrapped around my neck squeezing the breath from me. I grabbed my neck and when I opened my eyes I saw four young boys looking down at me. They were part of the Indian tribes that lived in that part of the jungle and the anaconda I thought was around my neck was a rope they had made from vines. They were laughing and poking me with sharp spears, enough that blood was running down my arms and stomach where they had struck me."

"I tried to speak to them but the rope was so tight I couldn't talk plus I couldn't understand them anyway. They kept motioning with their spears to get up and follow them but I was so weak it was hard to get up. They finally looped the rope under my arms and started dragging me through the jungle. I realized I had to get up or they would drag me to death, the thorns and bushes were already cutting me in a number of places. I tried to scream for them to stop but they kept on laughing and dragging me. When they stopped to climb over a log it gave me time to get on my feet before they started off again. We walked for hours only once stopping to drink from a small stream and eat something they had in a pouch. I went to the one holding the rope and motioned with my hands towards my mouth that I was hungry but he just laughed at me and kept on eating without giving me any food."

"When we began to walk again each boy would take turns holding the rope and every time the rope was exchanged the one giving up the rope would take his spear and jab me or hit me with the side of the spear and than they would all laugh again. When I stumbled they didn't care, they would continue to drag me until I found the strength to get up and walk. Once in the afternoon they stopped to rest and the oldest one came over to me and put his spear next to my thigh and made a motion like he was going to shove his spear inside me. I am glad he did, I can still feel the anger I felt when he did that, and it saved my life. The moment before that I was going to sit down and not get up they could drag me until they killed me, I didn't care anymore. But the anger inside that boiled over when he laughed about sticking the spear in me gave me strength that I never thought I had. When I got up I never stumbled again."

"Late in the afternoon we came out into a clearing with a few buildings scattered about. The boys paraded me around to all the elders and everyone poked and prodded me until the leader said something and then they took me to a pole by the pen they kept their pigs in and tied me to the post. I was kept there for six days; they fed me in the morning and at night whatever they had left over. In those six days every person in the village except one came around to pull my hair or look at my teeth. I only found out later when I could understand their language that I was the first person they had every seen outside of the jungle that weren't fighters or the few that came to plant. They had never seen a white person or a person with long black hair that I had at that time. I have the white skin of my father, his father was half white half Indian and I guess the white DNA all came out in me."

"The one person that never came around was the man I called the old warrior. In the six days setting in the hot sun I would see him sitting by himself away from the village. Sometimes he would be sitting and other times he would be standing. One morning when I looked over at him he was standing with his arms straight out and in each hand he held some kind of object. When I went to sleep that night he was still standing there with his arms straight out and the objects were still in his hands."

"The chief came to me on the seventh morning and untied the ropes that held me to the post. The rope around my neck he left on after adjusting the knot so I wouldn't chock if the rope were pulled. With him were the young girls in the village and he motioned for me to go with them. One of the girls grabbed the rope and yanked me to her side, saying something in the process."

"I had been given to the young girls of the village as there slave and they took full advantage of the opportunity. I was awaken before dawn every morning to do the cleaning and feeding of the pigs and the few monkeys they had. I was not allowed to eat except for what was given to me by one of the girls each day. Once while feeding the pigs I ate some of the half-rotten fruits meant for them. I thought I had hidden what I was doing but the next morning when the girl brought me my meal it was the fully rotten fruit that was going to be fed to the pigs. For three days that was all they allowed me to eat, from that day forward I have had no problem with eating anything alive or dead cooked or not cooked."

Shelby reached out and grabbed the bottle of water placed in the holder in front of her and drank half of the bottle before capping and returning it to the holder. Director Daniels only watched her expression as she drank from the bottle. After putting the bottle back she leaned back against the seat and turned her head to look out the window at the rolling countryside they were speeding past. They had been traveling for about an hour down the Turner Turnpike towards Oklahoma City and past a sign that said Wellston Exit two miles ahead. Daniels waited wondering if she would continue or if that was as much as she was willing to tell him. He had no idea and there was nothing in her file to indicate she had been in the jungle other than the small note that she had been found wondering close to a village that was less than a mile from the jungle when she was almost eleven. That meant she lived in the jungle for around eighteen months, wow.

Chapter 28

With her head still turned to the window of the car watching the scenery go by Shelby began to speak again.

"For the next five or six months, I lost track of the exact time, my routine was to get up before dawn, feed the animals, clean the floors where the girls lived, work in the fields and what ever else they wanted me to do. They would carry around these boards they kept flat on one end and sharp on the other, whenever I displeased any of them they would use the flat part of the spear and hit me. It didn't matter where they would just swing the spear and what ever part of my body was the closes, that's what got whacked. Some days my skin would be more blue than white from all the bruising."

"I got use to all of that but what was the hardest was being alone, although by now I could speak and understand their language, they treated me as if I was an animal. But from it I grew strong in body and mind and I knew someday they would not be able to stop me from leaving."

"The old warrior I spoke of was always there in the back ground. I never saw him talk or eat with any one else. But they had to have respected him for there was always food delivered to his resting-place on the fringe of the village. Each time I would ask one of the girls about him they would give me a look of hate and hit me as hard as they could with the board, but I never stopped asking. One day when I asked the one girl who had been the lease mean to me who he was she looked around to see if anyone was close. When she saw that no one could hear us she told me the story of the old warrior."

"She said before he father was born the old warrior had been a young boy from the village when a new group of Indians came through and asked their permission to plant a crop they called Cocoa. The village elders were given many gifts to allow the planting. For two years the plantings were done but the crops failed because of the soil the elders said. When the new group of Indians left the village they found that the old warrior and two young girls were also gone. They never heard from them again until the old warrior showed up on the fringe of the village half dead from wounds, he was by than a middle-aged man."

"After he was nursed back to health he told the elders of his captivity by the new group of Indians.

They had sold him and the two girls to people with white skins far down the mighty river. The old warrior said he never saw the two girls again. He was sold to a man who had a large cocoa farm like the one they tried to plant in the village, his owner sent him far away, across a great body of water to a place where the people had yellow skins and eyes that were half full. There he spent eleven years, until his eighteenth birthday, learning how to protect his master."

"When he was returned to his owner, he himself had become a master of the art of defense and killing in silence with only your hands. For thirty years he served his owner, training other men in the art of killing. One day the owner sent him to a small village to help protect the cargo of coca that was now refined into Cocaine. When he got there the village was burned to the ground and every person killed. The man in charge said his owner had given him orders to burn the village and kill the people, even the children, because one of them had alerted the police to his operations. Forty-one children were killed that day in the village and when the old warrior stepped foot on the boat taking the cocaine down river he broke down and cried. Then he killed every man on the boat before sitting it on fire and sending it adrift down the river."

"For a year the owner's killers chased him from one hideout to another, twice cornering and wounding him before he escaped. After the second attack he knew he would never be safe unless he went where they would never think of looking. Back to his home in the jungle that he had left forty years ago. But his owner had thought of that and a group of men were scattered throughout the trails leading back to his home. For two years he battle the group killing them one at a time until the last was killed with the old warrior getting seriously injured in the final attack. The old warrior has been in the village for twenty years now, the young girl told me, and their has been four attempts to kill him, one approximately every five years on the date of the burning of the village and the boat taking the drugs down river. The villagers believe it is now a battle of honor in which young men from the owner's area are recruited to attempt the kill. Somehow it has also become a code of honor that no village person will be hurt or killed when they come after him. His legend among the owners people has grown to God like status and the one that kills him will be blessed and honored for life, that is what the men who come after him believe."

Chapter 29

The vehicle they were traveling in sped through Oklahoma City and was entering Norman, Oklahoma home of the mighty Sooner Football Team that still holds the record of forty-seven straight collage wins. And but for Notre Dame's seven to zero win in the forty-eight game the record would have gone on for almost two more years. Daniels continued to keep his silence, he wanted nothing to interrupt Shelby from talking. Talking he believed for the very first time in her life about things that she has held deep within.

"Take the pity out of your eyes Jordan Daniels, I neither need or want it. Many lives have been worse than mine, in fact I feel lucky for the strength and knowledge I have received." Saying that, Shelby closed her eyes and was silent for many miles and Daniels let it be so as he to closed his eyes as they rode in silence. When she spoke again her voice seemed to be far away.

"After she told me the story she hit me hard a number of times with her paddle because I said I wanted to talk to him. No one was allowed to speak to him that was the law that was made after the first attack came to their village. I watched him whenever I could just to see and feel his presence. I watched his movements, how he walked and constantly observed things around the village and into the jungle. Many times I would catch him watching me from a distance until I could actually feel his eyes on me and than it became a game with me and maybe him also. When I felt his eyes on me I would quickly turn in the direction I thought he was and at first I would turn the wrong way half of the time. But one day, three times I felt his eyes on me and three times I turned in the right direction to find him. When I turned correctly on the third time in a row a smiled, the first smile I had ever seen from him crossed his face and he made a slight bow to me before turning and walking into the jungle. He did not come back for many days. For the first time in months my spirit soared, I felt I had a friend. "

'There were other times when I felt his eyes on me I would turn and he would not be there, that happened more frequently whenever he would leave the village for the jungle. At first I was disappointed and frustrated that I was losing that connection I thought I had with him until the day I realized I was always looking at the jungle not at any space in the village. That's when I starter concentrating very hard at the jungle and than looking deep into the jungle. The first time I spotted him deep in the jungle after I felt his eyes on me, I was overjoyed and I held one hand to my mouth as I pointed the other at him. But when I tried to look at him again after taking my eyes away from the spot he was at I could not find him. It took me many tries to understand that the eyes play tricks on you if you try and see something far away by looking directly at it when the object is well hidden. The girl with me would beat me hard with the paddle when I danced and pointed at him. They of course did not know that was what I was doing they thought I was trying to bring the evil spirit down on the village."

"Not long after I found I could spot him anywhere in the jungle, as deep as the light went. Than I began to mature, I had not yet started my period but my hips were beginning to widen and my breast began to form. In the village there was no rule or morality that stopped young girls and boys from engaging in sex until a girl had her first period. At which time it was taboo to touch her until her father gave his permission for her to go with another man to his village. It was a very casual thing and I witnessed it many times, as the young ones would have sex doggie style anywhere in the village, but only if they both agreed." Shelby turned her head sharply to look at Daniels.

"I'm sorry Jordan, am I embarrassing you?"

"No Shelby, you're telling me a story I have needed to hear for a long time and I believe you have wanted to tell for a long time." Shelby breathed deeply and only nodded her head.

"None of the young boys would touch me, first because they thought I had the evil spirit inside me and second because they thought I was ugly. Then one day it all changed, I was washing in the small stream that ran through the village when I rubbed the plant we used for cleaning our bodies across my breast. A sensation started deep in my stomach and raced to different parts of my body, even my lips felt the sensation. I was old enough to figure out what was happening to me but unfortunately the boy who had first put a rope around my neck and half dragged me to the village was in the water bathing and saw my reaction. When he walked by me he pickup one of the paddles the girls had laid on the ground and he used it to strike me across both breasts. To that point in my life I had never felt such pain shot through my body, he only laughed and walked away. "

"The next day the girls gathered around me and each took turns hitting me on my breast with their paddles, than they untied the rope that had been on my neck from the first day of captivity. I was overjoyed and through my tears from the pain of the paddles I began thanking them. The boys had been in the background watching as the girls beat me and took the rope off. When the girl threw the rope on the ground they turned to the boys and laughed. That was when I saw a new rope was in the hands of the boy that had hit my breasts the day before. He walked up and put the rope around my neck and turned to the other boys and told them they now had a slave and their job was to make me work hard each day."

"The next few months was a painful blur, they worked me before the light came up and into darkness. I was told I could eat what the pigs left in the morning. I was given no meal at noon and at night I ate what I could find when I cleaned the area's they ate in. When they caught me stealing food in the daytime they would beat me with the paddles, mostly on the back and butt. But the oldest boy always tried to hit me in the breast because he knew the kind of pain I felt from his blows. I learned to steal food without chewing by putting pieces in my mouth and letting my saliva dissolve the food."

"I could still feel the old warriors eyes on me and I would always turn and look in his direction but I stopped waving or smiling because when one of the boys saw me do that they would form a game with me as the object. The first time I waived at the old warrior the boys made me stand with one foot on the ground and the other tucked under my butt. Than they would put one stick in the ground in front of me and another one a few feet to the side and rear of the first one. They told me if I moved or fell before the shadow of the first stick crossed the second stick they would take me to the river and hold my head under water until one of the boys counted so many knots on a rope. That was one of the crude ways' they had of keeping track of time when it was to be for a short period of time. The time it took the shadow to reach the second stick was always an hour and sometimes two hours, for a while I always fell before the shadow hit the other stick."

"I learned fast how to hold my breath for long periods of time. The first time they held me under the water was because my leg cramped and I fell. I thought I was going to drown and I fought with every muscle I had to reach the surface. They were to strong and I could not reach the surface for air, I gulped water into my lungs and when they pulled me up I struggled for air until one of the younger boys took a paddle and began hitting me on the back. That night I practiced holding my breath and every night after that until I could go without air for over three minutes. From than on when ever they punished me by taking me to the river I would pretend to struggle after about forty-five seconds. In another twenty to thirty seconds they would bring me back up and I would pretend to cough and suck for air."

"When I stopped smiling and pointing at the old warrior and they had no reason to punish me they found the game they had started to be to much fun to stop. So they invented other games, taken from the things they had witnessed the old warrior doing, They would make me stand with my arms outstretched for hours, sometimes they would put something in my hands. If I dropped my hands they would beat me or take me to the river."

"Another game they played was one where I would race one of the boys down a narrow path. At the finish line was a rope tied across the path and as soon as the winner crossed the finish line the rope would release a plant that was tied to the end of another rope. The plant would hit the person trailing very hard but the sting from the plant wasn't to bad it was what the plant was made of. The sap in the leaves would leave large welts anywhere it touched skin and the skin would feel like someone had touched it with fire. The pain lasted for hours and there was nothing you could do to ease it. Every day for three solid weeks they played that game with me and every day I lost the race. It was hard to sleep at night with the feeling your body was on fire from everywhere the leaves hit."

"Because I couldn't sleep with the burning I would get up and go down to the narrow path and run and run and run until I was so exhausted I fell asleep almost before my body touched the hard floor. One night after I had ran once down the path and was running it a second time the finish line had been moved further down the path by ten yards. I went back to look at the old finish line to see if someone was there but no one was and I couldn't figure out why someone had changed it and I wondered why I had not noticed it on the first run. I took the three items that had been moved down and put them back at the right place and than jogged back to the starting line."

"Don't tell me, let me guess, the line was moved by the time you ran back down the path, right?" Said Jordan Daniels. Those were the first words he had spoken in a long time and he regretted it immediately, he had not wanted to interrupt a single word she was saying but the words just rolled from his mouth.

Shelby's eyes had been closed for a long time as she spoke, almost as if she was reliving the horror she went through at such a young age. Shelby turned her head to look at Jordan as she opened her eyes and a friendly smiled lit up her face as if she was thinking of an old friend.

"Yes Jordan, the line had been moved back to the same place when I finished my third run. That's when I knew someone was here and had just moved the line. I looked around in the darkness but could not see anyone and I did not feel his presence, but I was sure it was the old warrior who had moved the line. Walking back to the start I tried to think why he had done that but I couldn't come up with anything. I ran the path five more times that night as hard as I could and on the fourth run was when I knew why he had moved the line back."

"When I raced with the boy the first time I tried as hard as I could all the way but he past me because I became exhausted before the finish line. After that I realized I had to save some of my energy for the finish for the human body will use up the oxygen very fast when you are putting out one hundred percent. The results is a runner will run faster for the whole race if he starts out at only about eight-five percent, that way when you put on that last burst of one hundred percent speed your body will respond to it. I was getting faster each day but the boys also knew that and so they only had the faster ones race me."

"The old warrior was getting by body use to running the longer distance and it was building my stamina to where I could maintain the one hundred percent pace a little further down the path. The next night on my first run the line had been moved even further back and after twenty days the line was so far back that by the time I past the original line I was still going at one hundred percent of my pace. After the end of each night I would put the finish line back at the original place. By than the only boy that was racing me was the oldest and the fastest and he was beating me by only a step or two. Soon I knew and they knew I would beat him also, but I wanted to beat him before they stopped the game. I knew if they thought I could beat him they would not play the game because they were boys and girls should not be able to beat the best boy."

"For two days I pretended I was sick and I curled up and refused to get up even when they kicked me trying to make me get up the first day. Finally they left me alone the rest of the day and the next. Those two nights I raced all night and when they made me race the next day I pretended to still be sick and I fell half way down the path, they left me there until noon when they put the rope around my neck and took me to the river. Three times they punished me but I had become so good at holding my breath and pretending to struggle that they really though I was half dead when they led me back to the village for the night."

"The next morning at the usual time they led me to the path and told me if I stumbled or stopped they would rub the plant over my whole body. Oh Jordan! I never felt so strong as I did that morning lined up with him, wanting to beat him and the rest of the boys so bad." Shelby said as she subconsciously laid her hand on his knee.

"I raced down that path effortlessly Jordan, running like I was part of the wind, I beat him so bad I had time to slow down at the very end so that he could be close enough to get hit by the leaves. Afterwards I jumped for joy and screamed at the top of my lungs, which only made the boy's madder as they took me to the river and tried to drown me, I didn't care, I was happy. Twice after I struggled I let myself go limp so they would pull me back up but all the time I still had a lot of air left. I beat him Jordan, I beat everyone of the little bastards." As Shelby spoke her fingers felt like steel squeezing his knee until he had to put his hand over hers and pull it away.

"Oh Jordan, did I hurt you! I'm sorry, I should have realized what I was doing, I forget my own strength sometimes."

"I've never seen hands this powerful Shelby, not even in the great masters that taught at the Academy. One moment there long and soft, the next they feel like five steel rods sticking out of a concrete block." Jordan said as he rolled her hand over from front to back a number of times. She did not try to withdraw her hand as he spoke but Jordan released her hand when he saw those deep dark eyes trying to penetrate into his soul.

Chapter 30

Alex and Vera signed the last of the legal papers, it was done the notes were all in order, the company would be there's again in two hours. Poor old Chuck you thought you were smart, and I guess you were but sometimes luck or faith steps in and corrects things Alex thinks as they headed for their car and the meeting with Chuck Witt and his attorneys. The meeting was to be in the same conference room Chuck had used to stun Alex a few months ago when he ripped the company away from him and Vera.

Going south on Rockwell Avenue they passed one of the U-Store lots that held four hundred eleven million two hundred thousand dollars in boxes. They both turned their heads and looked at the storage area as they went by.

"This is kind of crazy Vera, here where driving past millions of dollars and we're worrying about our small company. Maybe we should forget about the company and take the money."

"What you're think is crazy Alex, have you forgotten what we talked about and who you damn well know is looking for it. I feel good we have made the money trail almost impossible for anyone to trace on the sixty million and as long as no one but a few at the company knows about the transactions we are about to do I feel we are safe. And even the ones that will be at the meeting will not know we own the companies involved, only that we have the power of attorney for the corporations that own the notes to the bank. But let me remind you, it wouldn't take a lot of digging to know who is behind the bank purchase. And one thing can lead to another with the finger pointing right back to us. Than the question will be how or where did we get that kind of money. Of course they will never find the answer to that last question because they don't know were to look."

"Except the people that lost the money?"

"That's right Alex, they are the only ones that would have the answer to where all the money came from. That's why we have to play it low keyed, no one outside of the two of us and the people involved at the company has any idea what is going on at our company. I will bet you a dollar to a donut that the people that lost that money have feelers out across the country in the larger banks and financial institutions looking for any large cash transactions."

"Besides all that money including the sixty million is going to be given to the Federal Government as soon as we can remove the sixty million from the sale of the company. Don't get greedy Alex, we will have enough money from the sale of the company that we can live off of the interest."

"I know dear, I just like to let my mind wonder on what we could do with all of that money."

"Right, let your mind wonder Alex right down to the jail house, if were lucky, if not you can wonder your mind down to some dark corner where they might and I mean just might find our bodies."

Alex and Vera stopped downtown at the Spaghetti Warehouse for lunch before the meeting with his old partner and the attorneys. With an hour to spare they walked along the canal that snaked through downtown Oklahoma City and Vera purchased a new purse she found in one of the small quaint stores tucked along the canal. It was a beautiful day and if they had more time Alex thought, they would take a ride on the riverboat that meanders down the canal to the Oklahoma River and back. But that would take close to an hour, maybe the next time they had free time that's what they would do.

As the appointment neared Alex and Vera drove their car to the parking garage next to the building. Stepping out of the car Vera reached over and took Alex's hand as they walked to the elevator that would take them to the conference room.

Jenny the receptionist greeted them both with a big smile and said how good it was to see them, but the big smile was a fake Vera could tell. The rumors were out that the Bell's were no longer partners in the company and the greetings from workers they past showed it. Some they had know for years avoided their eyes as they past while others gave a small smile and said hi as they past. Chuck Witt was waiting at the door to the conference and Alex could tell he wanted this meeting to be over with quick. Chuck reached out his hand to shake with Alex but Alex never volunteered his hand and for a second or two the silence hung heavy in the air between them. Diverting his eyes from Alex, Chuck smiled shyly at Vera and told her it was good that she came too.

Trying to ease the tension Chuck reached in his suit pocket and pulled out an envelope and half handed half shoved it towards Alex.

"You don't have to worry about a delay Alex, I have the cashier check right here for a little over a million dollars, you can take it now if you like, no need to wait until the paperwork is all done."

Alex ignored Chuck and pushed past him into the conference room holding Vera's hand as they came to the large round table. Nodding to the two attorneys that worked for Chuck and the three company attorneys

Alex and Vera sat down across from the attorney from the bank. Reaching across he shook the bank attorney's hand before nodding to the attorney that he had hired and who furnished the paper work to the bank.

Chuck came in a few seconds later with his wife Sara trailing behind him. Sara kept her eyes either on the carpet or her husband as she sat down across from Alex and Vera.

"Well, we all know why were here." Chuck began, "Here are the papers drawn up a number of years ago, as you can see the documents are all signed by me and Alex and as you already know today's date is the date stipulated on this final document signed ninety days ago. Now if you and Vera will sign right there where your names are typed we can be finished with this unpleasant episode and Alex and Vera can begin enjoying this fat check I have here for them." Chuck fumbled in his breast pocket digging out the envelope and laying it on the table in front of Alex. Alex just looked at it until Chuck with a nervous chuckle open the envelope and placed it on top.

"It's real Alex! Go ahead and take it, it's a cashier's check for god sakes Alex, it's just like cash."

"I believe my attorney would like to take a few minutes to speak to everyone if that's ok with you partner." Alex said, coming down hard on the word partner.

"Ah Alex, what's your attorney going to say that hasn't already been said in our last meeting, I know he wasn't here at that meeting, but did you really inform him of the facts, did you give him everything, all the legal papers?"

"Yes Chuck I did, now may he speak?"

"Shit, sure, why not, go ahead I have a few minutes I can waste before my golf game starts." He said with a half laugh as he looked at his attorney.

"Thank you Mr. Witt for the few minutes you so graciously granted. First I want to bring to your attention the exact wording of the documents signed a number of years ago by both Mr. Witt and my client Mr. Bell. Everyone is in agreement that it stipulates a ninety-day window in which either partner may call the options. Mr. Witt did just that ninety days ago and today my client Mr. Bell has two choices. One to take the offer agreed to in the agreement or two, to present the notes paid in full."

"For Christ sake we all know that get to the point your trying to make if you have one." Chuck said as he looked at Alex in anger.

"All right Mr. Witt, I'll do that. Mr. & Mrs. Bell which option do you chose today?"

"My wife and I chose the second option."

"What! Hell Alex you mean the first option, the one with the million dollar cashier check."

"No Chuck, I mean the second one. Mr. Moore your bank held the thirty million dollars worth of notes, who owns them now?"

"A Company called Black Industrials from Bulgaria."

"And who has the Power-Of-Attorney for this company?"

"You and your wife."

"What! What the hell is going on, Tom you're my attorney what the hell are they saying?"

Alex leaned over the table and got in Chuck's face. "Let me explain it real clear asshole, the table has been turned, you can take that million dollar cashier's check and shove it up your ass. The company is mine and you are out of here today!"

Sputtering and knocking over his chair as he tried to get up Chuck finally screamed again to his attorney to do something. But his attorney was already looking over the documents handed to him by the banking attorney.

"The documents are in order Mr. Witt, in addition they have been doubled stamped and doubled certified as to authenticity. As your attorney I have to advise you the company is now under the control of Mr. Bell and his wife. Unless of course sir you have thirty million dollars to purchase the notes."

"You stupid moron you think I have thirty million dollars stashed somewhere? They can't do that to me, we covered our tracks, you said there was no way he could do anything about it. You told me that a number of time! Do something! Get me my company back!"

He was still screaming to his attorney too get his company back, as the security officer escorted them both out the front door. His wife trailing behind crying into her handkerchief.

Turning to one of the company attorneys Alex handed him an envelope as he explained what was in it. "Bob there is a trust fund that Vera and I have funded for Chuck and Sara's three children. It's funded with fifteen million dollars; the amount each partner would have gotten if we had sold the company as planned. While you're with the company you will administer the trust through the company. The only stipulation is that neither Chuck or Sara will receive any of the funds and neither can have any say in how the trust is disbursed. If you leave the company the trust authority automatically transfers to the next senior attorney with the company."

That evening Alex and Vera had a quite but very expensive meal at the Deep Fork Grill in northwest Oklahoma City.

That same evening Jose Manual, one of Hector King's United States partners, also was dinning at a very expense restaurant in Houston. Only he was paying little attention to the exquisite food placed before him, he was giving orders to the vice-president of one of the largest banks in America to find his money. "Find the money trail," he screamed into the receiver, "its there somewhere."

Chapter 31

The vehicle was speeding down I-35 towards Dallas; it was just now passing Pauls Valley when Shelby broke the long silence spell. Jordan did not want to intrude on her thoughts; she had spoken through a lot of pain. For more than an hour before stopping and gazing out into the darkness of the speeding scenery. When she spoke again her tone was relaxed as if her thoughts were pleasant and she continued where she had left off.

"The next day after the race the boy I beat grabbed my rope and pulled me toward the river, I grabbed the rope and yanked. He was so off guard it knocked him down, I hadn't planned on doing that, it just happened. When I saw him on the ground and the looked of pure hatred on his face I knew he was going to kill me when he got up. Something came over me at that moment, I wasn't afraid of him or anyone else, I walked over to him as he got to his feet facing me and I kicked straight out with my left leg. My foot hit his testicles and I saw the pain go through his body so I struck out with both hands. I hit him below his left eye and just under his breastbone. I was stunned when I saw him fall to the ground and not move so I just stood over him until the other boys came running over. He was dead, they couldn't believe it and neither could I, but he never opened his eyes again." I had killed another human being and the only feeling I had was of relief that he would never again hit me in the breast.

"The next month was the worst time in all the time I was a captive, the boys would come at me two and three at a time to fight me, every day they did this and not once did any adult tell them to stop. Each day I fought I got better and better and it would take three and sometimes four boys to beat me up. The adults figured I was lower than an animal and the boys could do what they wanted with me. By now I was developing where even the male adults would ask me to have sex, the only thing that stopped them from taking me was their taboo about both partners having to say they wanted to."

"One day coming back from the steam where I had cleaned myself four of the oldest boys stopped me and told me they wanted to have sex and it wouldn't matter if I wanted to or not. They could take me if they wanted to because I was not part of the village or the people in the jungle. I tried to run but one of the boys caught the rope and yanked me down. When I landed I hit a rock the size of my fist and when the first boy jumped on me I grabbed the rock and swung it at his head. He cried out in pain and rolled away which gave me time to get up with the rock still in my hand. Then one of the boys grabbed me from behind while another hit me in the stomach. Swinging the rock I felt it hit flesh but I couldn't tell where but it gave me time to turn before the next boy tried to grab the rope. I hit him in the face with the rock and started to run but one of the other boys grabbed the rope and dragged me backwards until I felt something-hard press against my throat. It was one of the spears the boys always carried and he was bending me backwards. He was on one side of a large dead tree and I was on the other side as he pressed my back against it."

Jordan watched as Shelby's breathing came faster and her checks were turning rose colored, or at least he thought, the check facing him was turning that color. Jordan waited until her breathing slowed before speaking.

"Do you want to stop Shelby, you can tell me the rest of the story later if you like?"

"No!" She almost shouted. "No" she said more softly. "I need to continue for myself."

"The boy had me bent backwards over the tree as two of the other boys each grabbed a leg and lifted my feet off the ground. I've never understood why but the moment they grabbed and spread my leg's calmness came over me and it was like I was thinking in fast motion while everything else was in slow motion. That calmness has happened to me a number of times in my work, it is what has saved me from death many times."

"I know Shelby, I witnessed it last night, you did things that we are not suppose to be able to do. I don't mean to offend you but while I was watching you run I thought I was watching a large animal run, maybe a large cat I don't know. It freaked me out Shelby, you have skills that are not suppose to be associated with humans."

"I know Jordan, I think you will understand some of it by the time I finish, some of it I don't understand, I only know the old warrior believed all along I was different."

"When the calmness comes over me I can see things so amazingly clear. I saw the small movement of the boy holding my right leg, I knew he was going to relax his grip so he could grab under my hips and make his thrust. The moment his mind relaxed his grip but before his hand did I struck out and up with the ball of my foot and my heel caught him under the chin, when his mouth snapped shut he bit his tongue off."

"By than a number of other boys and even girls came running to the fight. The girls watched as the boys piled on until they had me spread-eagled across the tree. By than the small cloth, worn by everyone in the village, was gone and I was naked pinned against the tree trunk. They were going to have sex with me, all of them, not so much for the purpose of sex but because they knew I didn't want to and the power it gave them over me. But an adult carrying a spear moved the girl's aside and some of the boys. He looked down at me and said I was an evil spirit and I had caused trouble for the village. He lowered the spear until it touched the inside of my thigh than he told the boys I was unclean. He said he would thrust his spear inside by womb and destroy the evil spirit inside me. I could see his muscles tightening to push the spear inside when his eyes rolled back and he collapsed."

"Standing in his place was the old warrior, how he got there without me seeing him I didn't know but everyone moved back except one of the older boys that had his arms around my neck and head. The old warrior leaned over as the boy stood up and he put one finger on the boy and pushed. The boy looked like a mighty blow had hit him in the chest, he flew back three or four feet before landing on his back, his eyes rolled back in his head."

"The old warrior started walking to the center of the village but after a few steps he stopped, he did not turn to look at me but I could feel his mind telling me to follow. I tried to run after him but the rope was tangled in the tree trunk and bush. I frantically pulled at the rope and tore at the bush with my hands until they bleed and than the rope was loose, by than he was halfway to the center of the village. Running I came up behind him as he stopped in front of the chief, who was sitting in front of his house." When he spoke it was the first time I had heard his voice.

"This one has my spirit, she is part of me." "Than he turned and took the rope from my neck and laid it at the foot of the chief. Turning back to the chief and the village he spoke again." "You will treat her as you treat me from this moment on."

"When he turned and walked towards the edge of the jungle I followed behind until he spoke." "How can I teach you if you walk behind Tikwa." "That was the name he gave me, it meant 'Great Spirit'

"For the next three days he never spoke but he showed me how to eat and what to eat and he made me rest, really rest for the first time in more than a year that I had been in the jungle."

Chapter 32

Bill Mars was the best money could buy and very expensive. Ten days after the disappearance of the money Jose Manual had wired five million dollars to a bank in the British Virgin Island. The only instructions received, when Mr. Mars verified the amount was in his account, was the additional information of the description of Doug Ringo and Hernando Kling. His instruction in the initial phone call from Jose Manual stated he was to use his contacts in the Caribbean to locate any large amount of cash being transfer in or out of any bank in the Caribbean. It would not be an easy job with the secrecy all island banks were known for but Bill Mars was a highly respected Vice President of one of the largest banks in the islands. He was also very rich and wanted to get richer and the way to do that was to find the secrets hidden deep in all the banks of the islands. Not one bank refused to look the other way when millions of American dollars poured into their coffers. Bill had spread his wealth around very thick to the right people in the different banks and he knew from the moment that someone deposited a large amount of cash in any bank that the transaction had taken place and for how much. There were still secret accounts that he never found out about but he knew eighty percent of them within a week of the transaction.

Within a day, after talking to a number of contacts in the United States, he knew how much money Jose Manual had lost and it flabbergasted him. *How in the hell could you lose over two billion dollars and why did he have it all in one place?* Next, how could he get his hands on some of it, his regular fee for finding missing money was ten percent, that was a hell of a lot more than any measly five million he had been paid. Find the money first, than negotiate for the fee when you're in a much stronger position. It never once crossed his mind that if he found the money he would keep it. It never hurt to bargain but you never let your name be associated with being a thief, not in this area and not in this game.

For three weeks Bill Mars made contact with every know resource in the banking industry, but not one crummy lead came to light. No way who ever stole the money would try moving it all out of the country at once. Mars wasn't even sure they would move any of it out. The United States was a large country and there was a thousand places and ways to laundry the money.

But with that much money involved he continued to press every source he had.

When nothing came up after another three weeks Mars reluctantly distributed one fifth of the money received from Jose Manual. This money went to the wannabe's of the islands, these were people trying to get that one big break by furnishing people like Mars that one crucial piece of information everyone else had overlooked. Mostly the money was lost on a thousand different leads that only used up his time but he had learned long ago that someone out there knew exactly what he was looking for. They just didn't know it yet and now he was sitting in his office going over hundreds of phone, fax and e-mail messages from around the Caribbean.

Five days pouring over messages and verifying the information to see if it lead to any thing or disapproving the information quickly had Mars blurry eyed and his ear hurt from cradling the phone against it. After five days with a phone stuck to your ear it becomes pretty sensitive. All the phone and fax messages had been worked through and he was about a third of the way through his e-mails when he got what he thought looked like a good hit. A taxi driver had sent the e-mail from the British Virgin Island stating he had picked up a man at the airport and taken him to a restaurant a block from the British Virgin Island National Bank. The next day he picked up the same man at the Holiday Inn to take him back to the airport. Two things stuck out in the report that caught Mars's attention. The first was that the taxi driver said the man had two very large pieces of luggage when he picked him up. The second was that the taxi driver recognized him and was taking him back to the terminal that he had exited from but the man asked to be taken to the International Departure area and he carried no luggage except a small duffel bag.

It was funny in a way, when he read that e-mail, the man was talking about the bank that he was the Vice President in. Mars almost rejected the e-mail without further investigation because he was the one that people came to when funds needed to be discretely deposited. His finger was on the delete button when the thought came to him that maybe he wasn't so smart after all and that there might be someone else doing the same thing. If there was a man in his bank laundering money he had to be very good and very quiet about it. For in the eleven years Mars worked at the bank not one whisper had reached his ear about another employee laundering any assets.

Mars left his office at the bank and drove his car to the address he had written on a sticky note a few minutes before. The address was the home of Bob Atlas, the taxi driver who wrote the e-mail.

It was ten o'clock in the morning and Bob Atlas shift ended at eight that morning, Bill Mars had phoned before leaving his office and when a male answered half asleep he hung up. Now that he knew he was home it was time to get all the information the man had; he had also checked out the man earlier in the morning. It was easy to do now with computers connected into every corner of a person life. Mars knew the man was fifty-six, an American who came down on vacation twenty-eight years ago and never went back. He was a CPA or was when he came down but the CPA Board suspended him after he was found guilty of milking an old ladies trust account to the tune of three hundred thousand dollars. He also spent three years in jail for the crime and was deported back to the United States, where he promptly climbed on a plane and came in the back way through Mexico. For the last fifteen years he had been driving a cab and had kept a clean record so any authority that knows his record would care less if he staid.

Mars parked his car in the only spot that didn't have large potholes full of water. *Mr. Atlas doesn't* much *care where he lives* he thought. Most areas in the British Virgin Island have their slums but where Mr. Atlas lives is a step even below that. Spying a young boy on the corner Mars motions for him to come over to the car. When the kids reaches the car he took a five-dollar bill from his billfold and held it close to the boy. As the boy reached out to grab the money Mars pulled it back.

"You stay by the car kid, don't let anyone bother it, if the car looks ok when I return I'll give you another five." The boy didn't try to take the money again when Mars held it out; instead he leaned back on the back fender, reached in his pocket and withdrew a rather large knife.

"Nothin will happen to your car mister and I'll wait until you return to get my ten."

"Smart kid, I'll be less than half and hour."

No door was attached to the small house, just a screen to keep out the flies. Mars knocked on the wooden screen and waited, three minutes later hearing no one stirring he pounded this time and almost immediately heard a voice shout for him to knock it off, he would be there in a minute.

Mars watched a minute later as a man about six feet three with a bronze tan walked to the door. The first thing Mars did was hold up one end of a one hundred dollar bill to get his attention, and it did. He looked at the bill, than at Mars and than at the bill again before opening the screen door and walking back into the living room without seeing if the man was following him.

"You've come about the e-mail Mr. Mars?"

"How did you know who I was Bob?"

"Hell! Everyone on the island knows who you are Mr. Mars."

"I didn't mean it that way, how did you know to connect me to the e-mail you sent. My e-mail address and name that was given to you and others had nothing to do with me."

"Look around you Mr. Mars, how many people do you suppose have walked up to my door and flashed a hundred dollar bill in my face. I connected the e-mail immediately when I realized who you were."

"If you're that sharp Mr. Atlas maybe your e-mail has some truth to it. Why don't you start from the beginning and tell me why you think the man is important to me."

"No problem Mr. Mars. When I received that e-mail from a John Smith I almost immediately remembered the episode with the guy and the airport. When you pick someone up from the airport and their lugging two large suitcase and they asked to be taken to a bank your antenna goes up. Even thought he actually asked me to take him to a café across from the bank the address was what got my attention. But what really made me think I might have stumbled onto something you might need was when I picked up the same man the next day at his hotel. And he wanted to go to the international flight area rather than the flights to the United States and he carried only a duffel bag. Now that you're here I know my instincts were right."

"Mr. Atlas I'm a fairly good artist, please describe the man to me and I'll sketch as you talk." Bill pulled from the vanilla folder he carried a thin sheet of drawing paper. From his breast pocket he withdrew a drawing pencil and touched it to the paper and waited for Mr. Atlas to begin.

"Well, the guy was around six foot maybe six foot two, on the slime side, dark hair and forty-five to fifty-five maybe."

"Sounds like your describing yourself Mr. Atlas."

"He wasn't as good looking as me Mr. Mars." He said with a laugh. After going over the details of his face for the fifth time Mars handed the drawing to Atlas to see what improvement he could make to it. Atlas looked at the drawing and frowned.

"I see, your using me to verify the man, why didn't you just say so when you first got here Mr. Mars and saved us both a lot of time."

"I beg your pardon!"

"You already know who he is, that picture looks just like him."

"Are you sure Mr. Atlas?"

"Hell yes I'm sure, you couldn't have gotten a clearer picture if you had taken it with a camera. What! You telling me you didn't know what he looked like!" Mars looked at the drawing again before making eye contact with Atlas.

"I had no idea what he looked like Bob until you described him to me. So your telling me you could pick him out of a crowd?"

"Without a doubt I could pick him out, I don't forget faces."

"Bob is your passport still good and up to date?"

"Uh, yeah, the last time I looked it was, why?"

"You were a CPA at one time, right?"

"Was is right."

"But you haven't lost the knowledge of the trade?"

"You never lose the knowledge of the trade, Mr. Mars. You might not be up to date on the new laws but ninety percent of the stuff never changes. You add and subtract and hunt for the anomalies. When you find the anomalies you dig deeper until you find out why the anomalies happened. It's really pretty simple and it's also very hard to hide something if you dig deep enough."

"I'll pay you five thousand dollars a week plus travel to do some snooping for me, interested?"

"Five thousand a week, hell yes I'm interested, as long as I don't have to kill someone. What do you have in mind?"

"I'm not sure I have anything for you yet, but if I'm right I'll need for you to root around in the records of a certain bank."

"The bank wouldn't happen to be the one you're the Vice President of would it?"

"I'll be in touch with you in a few day Bob, give me your cell phone number please."

When Bill Mars reached his car, more than an hour after he had left it, the kid was still there. Bill stuffed two twenties in the kids ragged shirt pocket, pulled out two hundred dollar bills more and laid them in his hand.

"Kid, that house I just came out of, I want you and some friends to keep an eye on it for the next couple of days, if anyone comes or goes I want to know who it is. I'll drop by about this time in two days to see what you got."

"For two hundred dollars I'll cut his balls off if you like Mister."

"Nope, just do as I ask and the monies yours." Bill left the boy standing by the walk as he drove off, when he looked in his mirror the boy had parked his butt next to Bob Atlas's gravel driveway.

Chapter 33

Bill Mars spent the next week searching the bank files; he had already reviewed the film for the week in question and found the man leaving his bank. There were two good shots of the face of the man as he walked past the main teller area and again as he approached the outside door. Although it confirmed what Bob Atlas said the man looked like it did not get him identification of the man. So for the last week he had been running programs inside the bank computers trying to locate a large transaction by each officer but every one he looked at came out clean. There are twenty-three officers of the bank and Bill Mars had checked and double-checked every one of them. Nothing came up that could help solve his mystery of which officer laundered the money.

Next he spent four hundred thousand dollars to the top investigator in the Caribbean to find out every thing they could on seven of the officer. He thought for sure that one of these men would show additional funds coming or going from their accounts. When that failed he paid another four hundred thousand to have an additional thirteen checked the same way. Again nothing came up in the last few months although he did have ammunition on three of the officers that would put them beholden to him when he told them what he knew they had done. But of course he promised not to say anything to the authorities because they were part of the bank he loved so much and he did not want a scandal.

That left only the President of the bank and Jon Morgan, the little old grandmother. She had been with the bank almost from the beginning and he knew she was as strict as they came when it had anything to do with banking laws. He had remembered a few times she had cornered him in the hall and let loose with some choice words about his action with a certain customer and how the transaction should have been completed.

He called the investigator and paid the additional money for him to check out the President, he was not going to waste any money on her. When the investigator asked if this was the last of the officers he mentioned that the only other one was Jon Morgan and he wasn't going to give him any money when he knew he would come up empty on her. The man laughed and told him he would do that one for free.

Twice Bill Mars went back to Bob Atlas to see if he remembered anything else about the man and any conversation he might have had. He got nothing extra and was about to call Houston and tell Jose Manual he was dropping the case when the investigator call.

"You owe me big time Mr. Mars."

"I'll be damn, you found something on the President, you know he really was next to the last person I would have guessed was involved in something. I'm all ears, what have you got?"

"Jon Morgan, has she got a daughter named Rebekha?"

"Uh, yes I think that's her name."

"How about a grand daughter named Kailey?"

"Sure, I remember that name because it's one of my old flames, Jon introduced me to her some years ago, why?"

"When I had a name on a deed crossed checked in Jamaica it came up with the sellers as being Kailey Logan. Kailey Logan received the deed a few years ago from a woman by the name of Rebekha Hunt."

"I don't see where you're going with this, the last names are not the last names of either women?"

"Rebekha Hunt received the deed a number of years ago from Jon Morgan, now what got my pulse up was the names of Rebekha Hunt and Kailey Logan. They were involved in a number of other transactions over the years and I couldn't find any information on who they were or where they lived. So I went back and pulled every transaction I could find in the last twenty years on either name. Every real estate transaction went through the same real estate Company in Jamaica. The owner of that real estate company is Jon Morgan."

"Jon Morgan owns a real estate company in Jamaica!"

"Oh, and I finally traced down the two names, Rebekha Hunt and Kailey Logan. They work for a mortgage company in Hades and the Mortgage Company is owned by Jon Morgan's daughter and grand daughter, your little old grandmother has been funneling large amounts of cash for more than thirty years to her daughter and grand daughter."

"You have that documented?"

"Documented and on it's way to you via fax."

The next morning he was giving instruction to Bob Atlas to meet him at his office in the bank at ten o'clock that night. Once everyone had vacated the building he would let Bob in the back entrance to his office and he could work until approximately five o'clock in the morning running programs and checking out the paper work of everything she had laid her hands on in the last three months. In three nights he had a name to go with the face and the secret account number. The next night they found the wire transfer going across the ocean to Switzerland. Bill Mars still had to shake his head and laugh when he thought of sweet old Jon fooling everybody for the last thirty years. He would keep her secret, unless of course he needed her for something later down the road.

Bob Atlas held the fifty thousand dollars in his hands as Bill Mars explained what he wanted him to do.

"Bob, with your background you're the right choice, I want you to follow the money trail to Europe, find out who received the money, where it went and what their doing with it. This is top priority Bob; we have a very rich client that will pay millions to me if you get me the information we need. I'll split it fifty-fifty with you when the time comes."

The phone call that evening to Jose Manual got him what he wanted. There would be a man in Switzerland waiting for Bob Atlas, to lend a hand with the secrets of the banking laws he would run up against. With very large amounts of money placed in the right palms at the bank in Switzerland Bob Atlas was on a plane the next day flying to Western Europe. Money flowed to the right hands in the different cities and in five days he was flying back to the British Virgin Island with the name of Alex Bell.

Two days after his meeting with Bob Atlas, Bill Mars landed in Oklahoma City.

Chapter 34

Shelby had been quiet for some fifteen minutes, starring out the window of the car at the blackness of the night when Jordan Daniels suggested they stop at Gainesville, Texas to have something to eat. Half way through the meal Shelby's computer began to beep, telling her the search engine had found something for her to look at. With her meal half eaten she closed her laptop and told Jordan they needed to back track to Oklahoma City.

"Ok Agent Cruse, what did your program find that the whole F.B.I system missed?"

"Maybe your system never missed it because the programs you put in never asked the same questions I did." Jordan raised his hands in a fake surrender and wondered out loud what it was he forgot to ask. A large smiled filled Shelby's face as she spoke.

"I programmed the system to look at each city in Oklahoma and pull out everything that was out of the ordinary. Than I programmed the system to look at each of these anomalies in regard to money transfer or money laundering in any large amounts. The system noted three thousand four hundred and thirty seven anomalies. Nothing matched to anything else until the system ran a pattern check. Guess what it came up with Jordan?"

"You're the one with the information, you tell me."

"The first was the death of an unidentified man found at the Bethany Cemetery on Rockwell Avenue, apparently of a heart attack. The second was the abandonment of a large moving van in the parking lot at N.W. 23rd street and Rockwell Avenue, less than two miles away in a direct line of the Cemetery."

"You call that an anomaly, a man dies of a heart attack while visiting the cemetery and a moving van that was stolen and abandoned when who every had stolen it had no more use for it? That's pretty slim pickings Shelby."

"Your right Director that would be pretty slim pickings if not for the fact that the dead man had no identification and his fingerprints came back negative. That along with the information the moving van was stolen in Houston and I think it's something I'm going to look at. Now are we turning around and heading back to Oklahoma City or do I go alone?"

"Hell no you don't go alone Shelby." Five minutes later their vehicle was heading north to Oklahoma City.

"We have about a two hours drive to Oklahoma City Shelby, would you like to take a nap or bore me to death with the rest of your story about the old warrior?" Shelby turned sharply and looked at Jordan when he said that, only when she saw his smile did she realize he was kidding and really wanted to hear the rest of her story.

"Now that I've told you so much about my life I almost feel compelled to tell you the rest Jordan. I've never spoken to anyone about that life of long ago, not even to the people that adopted me. You're a good listener Director and I don't feel you judging me, I appreciate that. I know a lot of people think I'm a freak or that I don't have a soul or feelings. They could never understand the life I led or what pain does to your body and mind. When the old warrior led me away from the village and the rope was gone from my neck I felt so free and grateful that I would have fallen on a spear if he had ask it of me. I have heard you speak of your God Director, the old warrior was my God. He saved me from a living hell."

"It's hard for me to grab my mind around what you went through at such a young age Shelby, but something inside of you was stronger than all the pain and fear you went through. I'm a religious man Shelby and I have to think God was there with you how else could you have made it through those times."

"I mean no disrespect to your beliefs Director but if your God was there he is not a very nice one. I did not feel his presence within me nor did I ever call out for help. I felt alone and I knew my mind was the only thing that kept me alive." Director Daniels only nodded and closed his eyes as she continued.

"On the fourth morning the old warrior gave me a pair of leather shoes to wear, for a year I had worn no shoes and when I put them on they hurt my feet. Each shoe also had weights sewed into the leather that made the shoe weigh ten pounds. Every time I took a step it felt like I had cement blocks attached to my legs. He would not allow me to take them off, not even when I sleep. For a week I wore the shoes and when he motioned for me to take them off after the seventh day I knew for sure my feet would be a bloody mess. Even though as each day pasted the pain in my feet became less and less. When I removed the shoes I found that my feet and ankles had gotten stronger and not one blister was found on either foot."

"Each day at dawn I would put my shoes back on and walk beside him into the jungle as he opened my eyes to nature. Beginning in the third week as we were entering the jungle he reached down and picked up a stone that he placed in my hand. The stone was large enough that I had to spread my fingers to keep from dropping it."

"You must keep this stone in one or the other hand at all times, no matter what you are doing Tikwa. You must begin your training for their coming, the time is near."

"I asked him what he meant and why must I carry the stone and wear such heavy shoes. His reply was always the same. You must blend and become one with nature Tikwa, that is your destination, that is the spirit you have inside and soon they will come."

"Each day for weeks we would go into the jungle and each day he would walk faster and faster until we begin to run through the thick under growth. One day climbing a large hill I beat him to the top and only than did I realize I had not felt the heavy shoes on my feet. Nor had I felt the stone in my hand for it had become part of me. The old warrior knew what I was thinking and he took the stone from my hand and replaced it with a heavy stone axe he always carried at his side. This axe was carried by me until it was replaced by a heavy double edge knife a few months later."

"From the very beginning as we would walk or run through the jungle, when we came upon what he called a Pikne tree he would stop and make me use each finger to punch the trunk. When I had used all my fingers he would have me used different parts of my hand shaped in different ways to strike the trunk. Over and over he had me do this, but only to the Pikne tree. When I would ask he would only say that the trunk of the tree had the same strength as the human body."

"Pikne! I've never heard of such a tree?"

"I'm not sure that's the real name of the tree, only that it was the name the old warrior gave it. Soon I was beginning to puncture small holes with each jab of my fingers. One day I hit the tree wrong with one of the forms he had taught me to make of my hand and I cried and told him no one could punch a hole in the tree with that form. For two days we lived beside that tree without eating and drinking only what we could find of the dew on leaves. Two days he sat beside me and I listened as he explained the power of the mind. The power of the mind he said could concentrate all the body's forces to any area I wanted it to go. If I wanted to run faster I had to learn to focus on the running muscles in my legs, if I wanted the power to go to the tips of my fingers I only had to concentrate the body forces to them."

"When we awoke at dawn the next morning he told me to use the same hand form and strike the Pikne tree with great force. I was afraid to do as he asked me, when he had repeated it a third time I lowered my head and for the first time I said no to him. I was afraid he would be mad and send me back to the village but he only smiled and told me to listen."

"Watch the power of my mind Tikwa and believe." He said to me. He than walked to the tree, put his hand in the form he had taught me and struck out with lightening speed. His hand and two inches of his wrist were embedded in the tree trunk and when he withdrew his hand there was no injury to it."

"That freed the last strings holding back my mind Director, from than on when he said I could do something I absolutely believe it could be done."

"I do believe that Shelby, I have witnessed amazing feats of strength from people in extreme danger. The one that stands out in my mind was where one of my agents had over two tons of metal fall on him and his partner literally pulled the metal up more than three feet so another agent could pull him out."

"The first time I penetrated the Pikne trunk with my fist I turned and looked at the old warrior with pride in my chest. He half smiled and said 'Tikwa is becoming a warrior.' Those words filled my heart with such joy Jordan, I had pleased him and all I wanted to do after that was to show him the kind of warrior I could become for him. After that it was nothing but joy even thought he trained me day and night, sometimes going without sleep for two days at a time. The jungle had become my home, my security blanket."

"Than one day the games changed, instead of walking past the Pikne tree and hitting it we began running at full speed and hitting it as we past. The first time I did that I almost broke my wrist as my hand stayed in the trunk as the rest of me went flying by. If I wasn't hitting the trunk with my fist I was using my knife. Other times I would throw the knife some twenty to thirty yards from the tree and grab it out as I ran by.

Finally one day he told me to take my shoes off and he challenged me to certain distances. It was a big surprise to me when the first time I raced him with my shoes off he beat me. When I though about it later I knew he had been testing me, giving me little encouragement's by letting me beat him sometimes with my shoes on. But once the shoes came off he never again allowed me to beat him. I would have to earn the victory by beating him when he gave out one hundred percent. That time never came, no matter how fast or good I became. And with the shoes and weights off I felt like I was flying and my feet barely touched the ground as I ran. I was always amazed when he beat me for I thought of him as being a very old man until I really looked for the first time at his body. There was nothing but muscle on him and his hands felt like steel."

"Seven or eight months after he made me part of his family we went deep into the jungle for my final training, the time of there coming was close he would say and I was not yet ready. As we walked further and deeper where sometimes even the sun light could not penetrate he would point out the shapes of shadows and make me study them for long periods of time. At other times he would make me concentrate on him as he moved within and around large trees and tall leaves. I would be watching him lean part of his body against the curve of a tree or the elephant like leaves that grew abundantly in the jungle. He would wait until he saw me blink and when I looked again he would be gone, but he wasn't, he was still right in front of me only his body curved with the tree or the leaves until he was part of nature itself."

"You learned that well Shelby, I watched you at the Port of Catoosa as you blended in and out of the darkness. I think I'm beginning to see and understand some of the things I've seen you do, at lease it doesn't look like magic to me now."

"Magic! Why Director, you actually used the word magic. In your line of work that can get you killed quickly."

"I'm well aware of that Shelby, that's why it disturbed me so much when you first started at the Academy. Were coming into Oklahoma City, I'll call and make reservations at a downtown hotel."

"Ok, but first I want to go to the city morgue.
"

Chapter 35

Three men met Bill Mars as he stepped past security at the Oklahoma City International Airport all three were working for Jose Manual. As they departed the airport heading down Meridian Avenue one of the men handed Bill Mars a large sum of money and a rather large gun.

"What the hell is that for, I don't use guns, don't even like being around them."

"Mr. Manual insisted you have one Mr. Mars. He didn't want you to get in any kind of situation you couldn't get out of while working for him. He understands your reluctance to carry a gun but he would feel better knowing you aren't completely defenseless if a situation arises that called for restraining of a person or persons."

"I really don't want that things, tell Mr. Manual thanks but I've gotten along with out one so far in my life and I don't want to start now."

"Mr. Manual really insist you take it Mr. Mars." The man said as he handed the butt of the gun to Bill. Gingerly taking it from the man's hand Bill put it in his suit pocket as all three men frowned.

"Mr. Mars that gun will be spotted by every cop that passes you, please put it in the front of your pants or in the small of your back. Please keep in mind we are here to do any work that needs to be done other than your investigation. If you need any of us to do something just tell us and it's done, your job is to find out where the money is and nothing else."

"I already know where the money is, I told your boss that yesterday!"

"No sir, you don't know where the money is, you know who took the money as we do. But Alex Bell doesn't have the money in his possession. We've searched his house and office and nothing came of it, the only thing we do know is that he spent sixty million overseas purchasing different companies to be able to get his company back from his back stabbing ex partner. Of course, you furnished us with that information Mr. Mars and Mr. Manual will reward you well when the full amount is returned to him."

"Your job now is to get close to him, find out where he stashed the money. Mr. Manual has established a company that will show you as the sole owner and with enough assets to buy Alex Bell's company if he still wants to sell." One of the other men spoke up for the first time.

"You have five days Mr. Mars at which time Mr. Manual will use other means to find out where the money is."

Bill Mars had an appointment with Alex the following morning at ten o'clock in Alex's office. E-mails had been exchanged between the two with Bill explaining he had heard Alex Bell's company was on or had been on the market and he was interested in discussing a purchased with him.

Alex and Vera were at this moment discussing the e-mails received from a Mr. Bill Mars. Vera had checked out the name and found it belonged to a prominent banker in the British Virgin Island. That had caught her attention right a way, the British Virgin Island bank was where Alex had delivered sixty million dollars.

"I think were in trouble Alex, it's no consequence that someone from the very bank you gave the money to now wants to talk to us about buying the company. I told you the people who lost that money had the power to find out who took it, I think the time has come we call the police and call them tonight."

"Wait! Wait Vera, we don't know that for sure, you checked out the guy, he's the Vice President of the bank and has been there for a long time. His family goes back a long way in the islands; maybe, just maybe he really does want to buy our company. It was out there for sale for more than six months you know?"

"Alex you are so naive some times, I can't believe you said that. Were calling the police tonight."

"Let me do this Vera, let me talk with him in the morning, better yet lets both talk to him and see what he has to say. Meanwhile we can see if he has any information about us that he could only get if he knew about the money, or maybe he'll slip up and say something. Also we'll record the meeting with a hidden camera and watch it later to see if anything is reflected in his face when we ask certain questions. Is that agreeable with you?"

With a sigh Vera agrees with Alex to record the meeting and to be there to ask the right questions of him. But she could feel it in her bones, they were getting in over their heads and if not careful they were going to drown. After Alex had gone to bed Vera sat at the computer writing a letter, when she had finished she e-mailed it to herself at her mothers house. At lease the police will know why we were killed if it comes to that and she had fear in her heart that there was a very good chance it would happen. No matter what happens tomorrow she made a promise to herself that she was going to the police the next day.

Director Daniels and Agent Shelby pulled into the parking lot of the Oklahoma City Morgue at one thirty in the morning. Calling ahead Director Daniels had gotten a reluctant orderly to keep the morgue open until they got there. Normally it would have been closed to the public that late at night as Oklahoma City was pretty light on deaths that had to go to the city morgue at night. Walking through the front door and down the hall Shelby smelt the smell that always came from a place like this. It was almost a sweet smell, one that made you want to take a few quick breaths before continuing down the hall. A man in a white coat was standing at the end of the hall obvious impatiently waiting for them.

After shaking hands and introductions all around the orderly escorted them to the vault where the body was kept. Pulling open the door he glided the metal slab all the way out to its eight-foot length. Reaching down he pulled the sheet off uncovering the nakedness of the dead man lying on his back.

Director Daniels looked down on the body from the right while Agent Cruse looked down from the left. Director Daniels had gotten the first look at the corpse because the man was standing in front of Shelby when he pulled the sheet off. As he backed off Shelby got her first look and Director Daniels happened to be looking at her when she leaned over to look at the face of the dead man. Recognition, shock he wasn't sure but something out of the ordinary registered on her face for a full second before she got her composure back.

He watched her as Shelby begins asking questions about the man, she was again the detached Agent doing her job, but something had happened and he kept waiting for her to tell him.

"How did the man die?" Director Daniels asks the man standing next to him.

"Heart attack, he took his medicine after the attack but it was to massive, he died within half an hour of the attack."

"I'm finished here Director, do you need any more time?"

"Nope, how about you, anything about him ring a bell?" Shelby shot him a quick angry look before turning her head away.

"No Director, nothing, maybe the moving van will tell us something. I'll go look at it in the morning."

Walking back to the car the Director continued to wait for Shelby to tell him something, what he wasn't sure but there was something she was keeping from him. In the car she said nothing as she looked out the side window at downtown Oklahoma City. When they reached the hotel she was staying at he got out to open her door for her but by the time he was there she had already opened it and was standing by the curb.

"Why Director, still as polite as ever, sorry I forgot about that about you. Next time I'll wait in the car." She said with a slight grin letting him know she would do no such thing.

"Any thing you want to tell me before I leave for my place Agent Cruse, I'll need to complete a report before turning in?" Half-laughing Shelby mentioned that she had talked enough for both of them tonight. As she started to turn towards the hotel Director Daniels grabbed her elbow and turned her back to facing him.

"Who was he Shelby?" The first thing he noticed was the cold angry black eyes looking through him as she pulled her elbow away from his grasp.

"I'll see you in the morning Director Daniels."

"God damn it Agent Cruse, I saw that look on your face when you got your first look at him. You acted as if someone or something had struck a blow to your midsection. Now who the hell is he!" Shelby opened her mouth to say something before changing her mind and with a cold smile said.

"As I said Director, I'll see you in the morning." She left him standing there with his mouth open and the agent driving the car looking startled. *Shit he thought no one talks to Director Daniels like that, damn I had heard she had balls but that was something to write home about.* He quietly got back in the car and waited for Director Daniels to enter, which he finally did after five minutes looking in the direction she had walked and wondering if he should go knock some since into her or just have her arrested. He decided to do neither, but only because she had been honest with him up to that point and because of the help she had been. But when he asked her tomorrow she would give him an answer or she would be under arrest for obstruction of justice.

Sitting on the edge of her bed Shelby again saw the man lying on the metal slab, the man with the large ugly scar running down his face. The one that had sneered at her when he shot the mother monkey and tried to rape her the last night in her little shack. Tried to rape her with her dead mother lying five feet away with a machete stuck in her chest. Tears flowed as she thought of her mother and father and the horrible way they died, anger boiled up for the childhood she had or never had. The anger grew and focused on one man, Hector King. No one on this Earth was going to stop her from killing him with her own hands. No weapons would be used on him, he would see the wounds she could make in his body with just eight small fingers and he would see all of that before the final blow closed his eyes forever. For years she had pushed those thought away hoping the anger would go away with time but now she knew the anger was always growing and would never stop until he was dead.

Chapter 36

Shelby showered and put on clean clothes as soon as she had completed the information on Hernando Kling, by than it was six thirty in the morning. It didn't take long for the computer to spit out the name as one who had rented an U. Store unit a couple of months ago in Bethany, Oklahoma. Paying cash for one year's rental. Ringing the front desk she asked for a cab to be out front in five minutes. The rental document showed the unit was rented two days after Hernando Kling's death, which meant someone else, was involved in the stolen shipment. Both people he trusted the most were now dead, the two he trusted the shipment with. Could it be the one I mentioned to the F.B.I. his partner, Jose Manual; Must be she thought, he was the one that had the best chance of killing both men. Need to make a note to myself she thought, about how the man died, she was sure it was not a heart attack. But why kill one in one place and the other in another that doesn't make since unless one of them was in on it and he decided to eliminate any witnesses.

Hailing the cab she directed it to the U. Store unite on N. Rockwell in Bethany, Oklahoma. There was one of two things in that storage unit either drugs or cash and Shelby was betting on it being cash. Pulling up front she flashed her F.B.E. badge and told the cab to wait before getting out and walking in the front door of the office. A tall gangly man, with a nametag that read Mo Pierce was sitting at the computer when she walked in. She knew instantly how this man had to be approached for she had seen him look her up and down as she was opening the door to come in. but his eyes quickly went back to the computer as soon as he got his eyes full. He was more interested in doing his job than getting a better look at her. She smiled as she walked up to the counter and opened her billfold.

"Good morning Mr. Pierce, Agent Cruse, F.B.I. I need your help." She could actually see the man's backbone straightening as he stood to greet her. Leaning over he looked at the picture before looking her in the eyes.

"Yes ma'am, what can I do for you."

"A very dangerous man rented a U. Store from you three months ago, his name was Hernando Kling and I need to get into the unit he rented."

"Agent Cruse, I will be happy to help you but first I will need to see a search warrant issued for that unit. Do you have it with you?"

"No Mo I don't have a search warrant and I'll tell you why. I've been chasing this man across half the United States and I just, one half- hour ago, received conformation that he rented this unit. In another half-hour I will be on my way to the airport to capture him but first I need proof of what he left in the unit. If I don't get it I cannot arrest him and he will disappear again."

"You want me to let you open a unit without a search warrant!"

"That's about it Mo, I'll understand if you refuse, there will be no hard feelings on my part, I know you are just doing what you think is right. But Mo, sometimes what looks right turns out to be wrong. I need to get into that unit now!" Mo Pierce studied Shelby for a long time looking directly into her eyes; she never lowered her gaze from him.

"Ok Agent Cruse, if the F.B.I. needs to get in that unit than it has to be important." Mo sat back in his seat and typed in the man's name and the unit number came up. "Unit number 27 Agent Cruse."

"I'll need something to open the lock with Mo, do you have a bolt cutter around?"

"Yep, got to if you work here, hell a third of the people never come back for their stuff and we have to break in and sort through the stuff before we sell it. We go strictly by what the law say's we have to do before selling anything though."

"That I have no doubt Mo, I really appreciate what you're doing for me, this will cut a lot of hours out of the time I need to find him."

Mo reached under the desk and showed her the bolt cutter. The tool was a monster it looked like it could cut through an inch of steel. Following Mo to the middle of the first row of buildings he stopped in front of number 27.

"That's it Agent Cruse, do you want me to cut the lock off now?"

"Thanks Mo but I don't want you to get into any trouble if it ever came back that you cut the lock without a search warrant. That would never happen but there's no need to take that chance is there?"

"Sure, I understand, but ma'am I don't think you can cut the lock off."

"Thanks Mo but let me try it first." Shelby took the bolt cutter and with one push snapped the lock in half.

"Jesus! You must be God awfully strong, it takes me sometimes two, three times to do that."

"Just lucky Mo, I think I must have found the weak spot in the lock." As she got ready to life the door she stopped and turned to Mo.

"I'm sorry Mo, but I must ask you to go back to your office, what I hope I find here is not something

I can allowed you to see, you understand, don't you Mo?"

"Yes ma'am, I'll be in my office if you need any help, just holler."

Smiling at Mo as he walked back to his office, turning his head once in a while to look at her, Shelby waited until he entered his office before lifting the door. Standing there looking at all the boxes piled in neat rows that it made her wondered if maybe she had been wrong. There were not enough boxes here for a moving van to be used. Slipping a small knife from its hiding place under her right forearm she delicately sliced a five-inch square in the box that was eye level with her. Underneath was a Smokey plastic that hid the contents of the box. Puncturing the plastic Shelby pealed it back to expose packets of twenty-dollar bills. Smiling Shelby did the same with two more boxes before being satisfied that they all contained money.

I was right she said to herself as she smiled again. That's what the merchandise was and now the picture is getting clearer. All the drug money in the United States was being sent somewhere else and he used his two most trusted people to be the final delivers. What went wrong Mr. King, did one of them sell you out for more money than they could ever image they could spend? No wait, back up Shelby, the first man was murdered but the second one was almost to his destination before something happened. No, they were both betrayed by someone else, but who? The police report mentioned he had a heart attack, could he have killed

King's son, without a doubt if he thought he could get away with it.

Walking back to the office Shelby thought of calling Director Daniels but put her phone back in it's holder before she dialed, she decided she would wait a little longer to do that. Opening the door she stuck her head in and spoke to Mo.

"Mo, have you got another lock we can put on the unit until someone with a search warrant comes out?" Shelby handed him fifty dollars for the lock when he picked one up and handed it to her.

"Don't need any money ma'am, I'll give this one to you free."

"Mo do you work this shift every day?"

"Yes ma'am, Monday through Friday."

"What, you work seven to three?"

"No ma'am, I work seven to four, I get an hour off for lunch but I can't take it because there's no one else here to relieve me. That's ok though, they pay me for nine hours each day."

"Someone else must work the late shift than? The four to one shift?"

"Sure do, I had that shift once, liked it real well, because it's only four to midnight and you still got paid for nine hours. But I had to quit the nights, my little boy needed me at home at night."

"Did you find what you were hoping for Agent Cruse?"

"I got part of the clue Mo but I'm still missing some of the pieces, this will help a lot though and I really appreciate what you did for me."

"I was happy to do it ma'am."

"I know it's asking a lot Mo but do you think you might remember anything about Mr. Kling. How tall he was, his age, etc, etc, you know, anything at all."

"I wondered how good you were Agent Cruse and bet my self a trip to the movies with my little boy that you would ask me that question. Sure enough, I remember what he looked like, right down to his running shorts."

"Running shorts?"

"Sure, he came in without any identification. When I asked him for some he said he was going running at the park and had left his driver's license in his billfold which he also had left at his house. When I told him I had to have identification he said he remembered he had an old license from Texas in his glove compartment and asked me if that would be ok. I told him I didn't care what kind of identification he had as long as he had some. He ran to his truck and rummaged through something until he popped his head up with a driver's license in his hand."

When Mo finished describing the man Shelby again thanked him for all the help he had given her and she was about to leave when he offered another piece of information.

"Would it help if you knew what kind of truck he was driving Agent Cruse?"

"You know what kind of truck he was driving Mo?"

"Nope."

"No, than why did you just say what you did?"

"Sorry Agent Cruse, I was trying to be funny. I don't know what kind of vehicle he was driving but we can find out real quick."

"I'm listening Mr. Pierce!" her using his last name got his attention real quick and the smile left his face.

"Uh, what I mean ma'am, is that we have a camera that takes a picture of every vehicle that comes in or leaves our area. The film are kept for exactly one year, I know because it's my job to reuse the old film after one year."

It took less than five minutes for Mo to retrieve the film and for them both to look at it. The film got a perfect picture of the license plate on the back of the truck and a pretty good picture of his head coming into the area. The glare from his windshield made it hard to identify him but with enhancements from a special machine she would be able to see if he shaved that morning.

There were two boxes of film they carried to the office and when they returned the boxes to the storage area Shelby lifted the canister holding the film of the truck driver and slipped it into her purse. Within two hours she would have the picture in her hand of the man she was now chasing and his name.

Chapter 37

Renting a car Shelby drove north on Rockwell Avenue to the address she had written on the bottom of the picture she had received less than twenty minutes ago. One Alex Bell belongs to that face and she had his life history on three pages attached to the picture. There was nothing in his file to indicate he was associated with the drug trade or that he was ever around either King or Manual. But he sure was involved, because three months ago he had flown to the British Virgin Island for one day before going on to Switzerland and other European countries. The file didn't make since to her, how did he all of a sudden enter the picture as someone dealing in drugs. His life style said different, his wife and kids said different and yet he stashed millions of dollars of Jose Manual's drug money for him in Bethany, Oklahoma.

Shelby entered Alex Bell's house at eleven o'clock in the morning after finding no one around. Taking less than half an hour she had searched every room in the place and found nothing. Even his house said different, what the hell was going on did they hire him just for this job? Start from the beginning Shelby, walk your self through it, find the link, its there somewhere.

Walking to the big building in the back of the house Shelby again had no trouble getting in. In five minutes she found three crumbled up bank markers that designated they had been wrapped around ten thousand dollars in one hundred dollars bills. In addition she found large black tire tracks, Very light but definitely large tires from a truck. Finding white markings on the floor she went down on one knee and starter reading the numbers Alex had made that first day, the numbers confirmed her suspicion that there was more money somewhere in the city, a lot more. Finding nothing else she walked back to the house.

Finding a computer in the office he kept at home Shelby downloaded the contents including everything they wanted kept secret. The special little machine she carried took less than three minutes to complete the down loading. Taking a picture of his wife, Shelby exited the residence the way she entered. The front door had been easy to pick and no one would know she had been in the house.

Driving to downtown Oklahoma City Shelby thought about Hernando Kling and his roll in the whole thing and that was when the pieces fell into place. He was a vicious man and when he saw the one opportunity in his life to be wealthy beyond his imagination and to stick it to his boss at the same time he took it. He killed Doug Ringo, King's only son and the man in power over him. He had to have enjoyed that killing knowing what it would do to King but he also had to make sure he disappeared with the money. His plan could have been to continue up the road to the Port of Catoosa where he would off load the money before killing the Captain of the boat. Or he could have planned to stash it somewhere else and disappear with enough to buy him out of any trouble he might come across. His plan had to be one that included making Hector King think he also was dead.

On second thought, that makes the boat thing wrong, Hector King would have known he made it to the boat, so that was out. But whatever his plan was it backfired, because he had a real heart attack and died somewhere in Oklahoma City and our jogging friend must have come across him. That's the only explanation for Alex Bell to be involved in any of this.

Alex Bell shook Bill Mars's hand and introduced Vera as the three walked down the hall to Alex's office. The small talk lasted five minutes or so before Alex got to the point.

"Mr. Mars how did you hear about our company being up for sale?"

"I'm a banker Alex, I knew six months ago you and your partner was serious about selling your company. When a couple of the big boys came calling on you I figured my group never had a chance, so I never contacted you. But when nothing happened for six months I thought that would be a good time to give you a call. That was after I determined you weren't in any negotiations at the time. And please, call me Bill."

"What kind of financing do you have Bill? What price have you settled on that you think the company is worth?"

"Vera I really wouldn't have any idea what your company is worth until our accountants looked over your last three years of audited and certified financial statements but I like the concept your company has. And I feel it would fit in nicely with the companies we already own."

"As for your question of financing, I'm sure you have already checked that out and if you have any questions I will be happy to discuss them with you."

The three discussed different aspect of the company and financing for the next hour before Vera mentioned they should finish the discussion over lunch down by the river walk. She mentioned there were a number of great restaurants where they could sit outside and not be disturbed or overheard.

Vera mentioned it was a brisk seven-block walk to the restaurants but it was a mild day for July and Bill might like walking past the Oklahoma Memorial

on the way. Alex vetoed the idea and instead hailed a
cab for them as they left the building. Vera decided
to treat Bill to the hospitality of Oklahoma eating as
she directed the cab to the location she wanted. Alex
gave her a frown when she guided Bill into the Stumps
Burger House along the canal. When the waitress came
she ordered the B.B.Q. plate for each of them, telling
them she had eaten here before and this was the best
in town.

Puling her car into the parking lot of the Copermark
Bank Shelby found a space that had her car heading
directly for the Journal Record Building where Alex's
office was located.

With the pictures of Alex and Vera in her front seat
Shelby relaxes in her rented car. She had called, on the
way downtown, Alex's company to see if he was in.
She was told he was but both he and his wife was in a
meeting and would not be available for the rest of the
day. If she would leave a name they would return her
call as soon as they had the time. Shelby thanked her
and hung up without giving her a name. The only thing
she wanted to know she got, they were in their office.

Shelby had planned to wait where she was in case
they came out until around four. At that time she
would drive back to Wiley Post Airport and make a
call to Director Daniels. But less than half an hour later
she spotted them coming out the front entrance of the
building with a third person. Grabbing her purse she

tried to extract a small but very powerful camera before they entered the cab but she was too late. She waited until the cab pulled away before following them to the Bricktown area of the city.

This area use to be nothing but old red brick warehouse's until the city fathers came up with a plan to rejuvenate the downtown area with a program called Maps 1. To do that they put forth on the ballot for the people of Oklahoma City a one-cent sales tax to pay for the projects. The people of Oklahoma City passed the plan by a seventy-five percent majority, which surprised everyone involved. The Maps program was passed in the nineties and by the year 2003 the whole downtown area was being remade. Keeping the red brick façade the theme went throughout. The program was so successful that the people voted again to extend the sales tax for another five years in the second program called Maps 11. It too was a huge success and the city now had a canal running through the heart of downtown and out to the Oklahoma River. Billions of dollars in development flow in from the private sector, making Oklahoma City a destination for thousands of visitors. The first attraction of course was the Oklahoma Memorial built after the April 19, 1995 bombing that killed one hundred sixty eight men, women and children. The dreadful part of the act, beyond the killing of the innocent men and women, was that the truck bomb was parked almost beneath the day care center and ended the lives of so many young children.

Shelby watched, three cars behind, as the cab dropped the three off at the corner of Bricktown only half a block from the restaurant. Shelby found a parking space, placed her quarters in for the maximum hour allowed and walked to the entrance of the river walk with her camera in her hand. Walking down the second walkway she had gone only half way when she spotted the three on the same level across the canal sitting at Stumps Burger House. Discretely taking the camera from her pants pocket, leaving it close to her stomach which made it look like she was not taking pictures, she took several pictures as she walked past. At the end she took a chance and raised the camera to her eye and took three quick pictures of the other man sitting with Alex and Vera. This man was new to her and she needed to know who he was.

Shelby returned to her car and attached the memory card from her camera to her computer. The pictures would reach the person within five minutes and she was sure that by late afternoon she would have the identification of the man having lunch with the Bell's. After that was done Shelby found a position she could discretely watch the three, an hour later, their meal completed, she watched as the unidentified man shook their hands and left. Alex and Vera sipped their drinks for another fifteen minutes before leaving the restaurant and walking back to their office.

Shelby decided to follow on foot, watching them from some fifty to sixty feet behind. They looked like a couple that loved and respected each other even after twenty some years of marriage. Shelby liked that she wondered what it would be like to love a man for that long, to know his mind and body almost as well as her own. A light sadness settled in her as she thought of that, what would it be like to lay with a man, a man you loved. To open up and let him explore your body as freely as he wanted, to rest in his arms afterwards smelling the spent passion covering their bodies.

Shelby had loved but not that kind of love. She loved the old warrior and would have died for him without questioning why. She had never made love to a man or had a man make love to her. Although she had numerous opportunities something deep inside keep her from taking that final step.

Shelby followed the couple into the building and decided to get close to them when she saw they were heading for the elevator. She timed it so that the doors were beginning to close when she walk in, they were the only three on the elevator and Shelby smiled to herself when she saw the reaction between them. Looking at Alex she saw him look her up and down before directing his eyes to her face and when they made eye contact both gave a small smile before he looked away. What made Shelby smile was the smile on his wife's face as she noticed her husband looking her over, it was a smile of acceptance without a trace of jealousy they were very conformable with each other and her smile told Shelby a thousand things about their marriage, all good.

Shelby waited until they both exited the elevator before hitting the button for the ground floor. When she reached her car she flipped open the laptop and scanned for any information from her contact. Nothing had come in yet so she settled down in the seat of the vehicle and watched the building.

At three forty- five her laptop dinged, telling her she had an incoming message. The picture she sent came back with a name and it raised her eyebrows in concern. What was this man doing here so far away from his place of business, had someone sent him to find out about the Bell's? He was into a lot of things in the islands but no hint of anything to do with drugs or drug money. Wait! Don't be so fast on dismissing him with drug money, the island was notorious for laundering money from drugs. And he was a Vice President of a large bank, maybe he's been smart in his dealing and no one's pointed a finger at him. If so, what is he doing here? What would he know about the Bell's unless-----shit, of course, they've found him, they know who took the money. He's been sent to extract the information on where the money is, but he's not the one that will do the dirty work. He's got partners around somewhere in the area. Did they spot me? Shelby slowly scans three hundred and sixty degrees using her hand mirror; she could detect nothing out of the ordinary with the people around her.

Pulling her car out of the parking lot Shelby headed for Wally Post Airport taking a round about way and also doubling back a few times to see if there was a tail on her. If anyone was following her they were good because she detected not a single vehicle following her for more than a few blocks.

Coming to a stop in the parking lot of MGM Inc. she nosed the car east so she had a clear view of the U-Store. Pulling out her field glasses she focused on the U. Store office, inside she found what she was looking for. Mo Pierce was not on duty, the woman had replaced him for her shift, that was good, for she didn't want Mo there to mess up the works. Shelby flipped open her cell phone and called Director Daniels. It was four thirty-eight and a little later than she had wanted to make the call but it couldn't be helped she had to make sure no tail was on her.

"Director Daniels." Shelby took a deep breath before speaking.

"Hello Director."

"Agent Cruse! It's nice of you to call, where the hell have you been, we had an appointment this morning!"

"Yes sir, sorry about that Director maybe I can make it up to you?"

"Make it up to me! All right Cruse I'm listening but it had better be good, because your ass is in hot water and I will remind you that you are a guess of the United States."

"Can you get an open-ended search warrant right away?"

"Yeah! I can get an open-ended search warrant, how soon do we need it?"

"Now!"

"Now?"

"Yes sir, right now."

"Name and address."

"5920 N. Rockwell unit #27, Bethany, Oklahoma."

"Name of the person occupying apartment #27?"

"It's not an apartment Director, it's a U. Store complex."

"A storage company?"

"Yes sir."

"You found the merchandise?"

"That's what I hope you will help me find out Director."

"Alright Agent Cruse, give me the name."

"Hernando Kling."

"Hernando Kling! The second driver of the truck?"

"The one and the same Director."

"Where is he now, will he be there, do you have him under surveillance?"

"You made contact with him early this morning Director."

"I made contact with Hernando Kling early this morning! Explain Agent Cruse just how I could have made contract with this man early this morning when

I was with you for---------the man in the morgue was Hernando Kling?"

"Bingo Director, you win the prize."

"Now I understand your reaction Agent Cruse, but that doesn't excuse you for keeping information from me for more than fifteen hours. What have you been doing in those fifteen hours?"

"Can we put a hold on that Director until after we find out what's in the storage unit?"

"I'll be there in forty-five minutes Agent Cruse, I'm assuming your already there and we won't have to wait for you?"

"I'm across the street Director." The line went dead before Shelby could say anything else. *Gee, I think the Director is peeved with me* she thought smiling broadly.

Chapter 38

Forty minutes later Shelby watched as three vehicles raced north on Rockwell Avenue towards the U. Store building. Why don't you let the world know your coming she thought as two cars made sharp right turns into the entrance while the third one made a sharp right turn into the exit, effectively blocking incoming and outgoing vehicles. Three minutes later she pulled up behind the vehicle blocking the exit and watched as the frighten woman working the desk was backed up against the wall talking as fast as she could while six agents stood close with hands on hips which exposed the weapons they carried.

All six agents turned towards the door when Shelby opened it, only Director Daniels acknowledged her presence. Shelby noticed they had come prepared, one of the agents carried a bolt cutter even bigger than the one she had used earlier.

Standing by the storage bin Director Daniels nodded to the agent with the bolt cutter and in one swift motion he cut the lock. Another agent slid the door up exposing the boxes inside, including the neat little squares cut out of a number of the boxes in front. Director Daniels walked over with Shelby and stuck his hand in one of the open squares and pulled out three bundles of fifty-dollar bills neatly wrapped in ten thousand-dollar packets. Turning to one of the agents he motioned him over and whispered in his ear.

"Get the bean counters out here and you and your partner say with the money until they arrive. You and your partner will stay in full view of each other until they get here you understand that? It's for your own security John, nothing against either of you but I want no chance, with this large amount of money, that someone comes back later and tries to second guess us on who was here and for how long."

"What do you make of the neat squares cut in some of the boxes Director?" one of the female agents asked.

"Hard to say, maybe they wanted to identified which boxes had what kind of bills, maybe they just wanted to look at the money, who knows." He said as he looked at Shelby.

"Bob drive my car back, keys are in the vehicle I'm going to let Agent Cruse drive me back to the hotel. Let me know when they get a count, ok?"

"Will let you know as soon as they finish Director. Have a pleasant night." The remark went straight over his head but not Shelby's. She knew what the agent was thinking about and so did the rest of them as she saw the faint smile on both of the female agents.

"I'm hungry Agent Cruse, turn left on thirty-ninth expressway there's a Panera Bread a couple of miles away, I love the bowl of soup they make out of bread. Anything at the storage unit that strikes you as odd Agent Cruse?"

"You mean other than the neat square holes cut out of some of the boxes?"

"No, I know who did that Agent Cruse."

"And how do you know who cut the holes Director?"

"That's what I would have done if I had gotten there first."

"Are you accusing me of doing the cutting!"

"Was there anything else that looked odd Agent Cruse?" Shelby turned and looked at the Director but his face was quite and he was watching the traffic on his right side.

"The amount of money, although there's a lot of cash you wouldn't need a moving van to carry it."

"Right, there's more money hidden, I'd say two or three times that much."

"I agree Director, now all we have to do is find out where Hernando Kling hid the rest." The Director turned and looked at Shelby hard before speaking again. She noted the tone in his voce.

"Hernando Kling didn't hide the money, he was dead two days before the storage bin was rented. I'm surprised you missed that Agent Cruse." Shelby kept her eyes on the road as he continued to speculate about the money and who might have hidden it, never once taking his eyes from her face.

"Turn left at Portland."

"What, I'm sorry, what did you say Director." Shelby had tuned him out when he started talking about who might have hidden the money and why, she had let her mind wonder to the old warrior.

"Turn left at the light and go about a mile, than back right for a quarter mile, the restaurant is on the left across from Baptist Hospital."

He told Shelby to find a table on the outside and he would go in and order for the both of them. She told him to get her the same thing he was ordering; she wasn't much in the mood for food although she was hungry. But hunger played a very small part in her mind; she had been hungry, near starvation for so long when she was nine and ten that the pain was little noticed now. She would make the motions and feed her body the nourishment it needed when it needed it, but a little hunger pain was not a signal that she needed nourishment yet.

Director Daniels walked back to the table and placed a walnut salad and a bowl of black bean soup in front of Shelby, the same thing he placed before himself. They ate in mostly silence with the Director bringing up a subject now and than but when he got little response from Shelby he stopped and they both finished the meal in silence. When Shelby pushed her half-finished plate away he excused himself and went inside. A few minutes later he emerged with two large frosted glassed of tea which Shelby thanked him for saying that was just what she needed something cool.

"I'm curious Shelby, did you ever find out what the old warrior meant when he repeated the statement that the coming was near?" Shelby sat sipping the tea for a long time while looking over at the medical helicopter perched next to Baptist Hospital. They watched as the medical nurse lowered the small baby into the waiting arms of a second nurse who than ran towards the emergency door of the hospital. The Director thought she was not going to answer and was getting ready to tell her to take him back to his hotel when she spoke.

"Yes Director, I found out what he meant. I found out right after the episode with the Black Panther."

"Black Panther!"

"Yes, we had been in the jungle for almost a month this time, watching every animal we came across. We didn't just watch an animal for a few minutes, we never take our eyes of the animal we had chosen, and sometimes we watched for twenty-four hours. When you watch an animal for that long with such detail you begin to think like that animal and anticipate where it would be going and what it would do."

"That day we stood beside a clump of trees with tall grass all around. The tall grass was unusual for that area of the jungle but the trees grew so that a large amount of sunlight hit the ground. Within minutes I saw the markings of a large cat and that was when the old warrior told me I must follow the Black Panther until he does not know I am there. When that is done I must stock and kill the same kind of animal in the same way that I witness the last kill by the Black Panther."

"That night the Black Panther left it's den and roamed the jungle looking for a meal. Three times he turned his head in my direction and snarled, letting me know he knew I was there. On the eleventh night he only turned his head once and looked at me, but he did not snarl. In the day when he would sleep the old warrior would make my mind go over every move the Panther made. He would make me describe the muscles in every section of his body and how they moved when he walked, ran and most important when he made a kill."

"When the Panther first left his den each evening the old warrior and I would be close by in the open so he could see us clearly. We would be separated by thirty feet on the trail he always took to begin his hunt and he would walk less than ten feet from each of us. When he passed the old warrior each time he would give a low growl but when he passed me it would be much louder.

I asked the old warrior why the two different sounds and he told me the Black Panther could smell my fear of him and it was a warning that he was telling me he could kill me if he wanted to. The sound to him, the old warrior said, was a greeting for he smelled no fear in him. Two weeks later I was following behind him when he gave that low greeting sound and I thought it was for me but a few seconds later a female Panther came to him. I watched them mate many times that night.

The next night as we were standing by the trail he gave the low greeting to the old warrior." The Director was listening, enthralled with what he was hearing, when her voice changed to a flowing melody.

"When he passed me he stopped and gave me that low greeting, I was so thrilled and shocked I almost screamed. He walked completely around me letting his body slightly touch my bare legs and when he got beside me he raised his head and looked directly into my eyes with the most beautiful yellow eyes I had ever seen." Shelby let out a half-laugh giggle before she said.

"Than he raised his leg and pissed all over my lower body." Shelby's eyes were glowing and she doubled over in laughter for a full minute before she could get herself under control and the Director was laughing along with her, not knowing why but laughing because she was laughing and he loved her laughter. .

"He pissed on me Jordan, that big beautiful cat marked its territory all over me! The next three days and nights were wonderful, the old warrior taught me by day and the Panther taught me at night how to kill. I would watch the muscles in his back legs and they were doing the same thing that the old warrior had taught me. Concentrate your mind to send the energy to one part of your body, his muscles would almost look like waves going back and forth before he leaped."

"I was so happy and proud, I though I could do anything and it took a beautiful animal to teach me the best lesson of all. The Panther had allowed me to follow him a few steps behind when he went on his hunts and one night feeling like I was the king of the mountain because I was so close to him that his tail would brush me as it went back and forth."

"We both crouched in the attack position as we saw the monkey on a low branch at the same time. When I knew he was making his leap I also leaped, but I leaped a fraction of a second before I thought he was going to, but he saw something I had not. The monkey was turning its head in our direction and if we had stayed still until he turned his head back the Panther would have made his kill. Instead I leaped and he didn't, I flew over his head as the monkey climbed higher in the tree. I rolled to a sitting position three feet in front of the Panther, his big yellow eyes were looking down at me and I could see the question he was trying to answer in his mind. Making his decision he lowered his head a few inches towards me and showed me his fangs, all three inches of them, he never made a sound. Than he turned around and walked away from me. After recovering my shock and being put in place for thinking I was so good I took off running and finally caught up with him. And to let me know he hadn't forgotten, every time I got close enough for his tail to brush me he would swing it hard and half knock me down. The next night I made my kill of a monkey attacking up the tree just as I had watched him do. I than laid the monkey at his feet as a gift and he took it to his female."

Chapter 39

Director Daniels left the table to refresh their teas as Shelby sat staring off into her own world thinking about the big Blank Panther. He shook his head thinking how could anyone relate to what she has been through and how did she ever turn out the way she has. Maybe the old warrior was right she was born with that special spirit inside. She has a brilliant mind, could have been anything she wanted to be but her childhood formed her core feelings and beliefs, things that no other human could have experienced or endured. Now he could almost understand what he saw on the ship a few days ago but something else was still missing, something cold and dark and hard within her soul. He hoped he could understand, maybe by just listening he was helping her, he knew she had not spoken those words to another human. And her laughter and smile, he wanted so much to see her laugh and smile, he knew she did it very seldom.

Placing the refreshed tea in front of Shelby he sat and watched her for a few minutes, she was at that very moment running somewhere through that jungle of hers, he could see it on her face.

"You were going to tell me what the old warrior meant by the coming was near Shelby." Smiling and nodding her head she half patted half hit the hand he had used to touch her elbow when he spoke.

"He was showing me a new form for my hands to punch through a smaller Pikne tree trunk when I asked him again why I had to know all these forms."

"The coming is near Tikwa the crops are in it is very near."

"What coming I said, what coming are you talking about?"

"When the fifth cycle of crops are finished they will come seeking glory and prestige. Many years ago I killed men for the master I worked for. His trade was evil for he would send many boats full of drugs to other countries to inflict pain on the poor people who used. One day I turned against him, killing his men and burning his boat full of drugs. I knew he would send men after me to either bring me back for him to kill in his special way or to kill me if they could not bring me back. I escaped through the jungle to my old village thinking they would never think of looking for me here. I was wrong for they lined the trail all the way back to my village to catch or kill me. The men they sent the first time were not experienced in jungle killing and I killed them all one at a time on my way back to the village."

"When my master found out about it three years later he offered an award of one thousand acres to the man who brought me back dead or alive. In the fifth year enough men had signed up that he furnished each with a small amount of money and material to make the one-month journey. Eleven made the journey that fifth year none came back from the jungle around the village. The master died four years later but left a will that offered the same one thousand acres and a small amount of cash and material to each man who would agree to go."

"The men that signed up this time were seeking glory and prestige, not the acres or the small amount of money and material. For in the ten years the legend that I was a great sprit warrior grew beyond rumors to a truth. They believed if they killed me they would take my spirit into themselves and become someone people would worship. Twenty-three skilled hunters made the journey the next time but none returned."

"In the area were my master lived they are now worshiping me as a spirit god and men train up to five years to prepare to fight me. The cycle has not changed for a long time, every five years a new group of fighters seek glory by hoping to be the one that kills me and take my spirit back to their land. It is a cycle that cannot be broken until my death."

"I tried to tell him we could leave the jungle Jordan and live so far away they would never find us but he would not listen. He would only say that wherever we went they would find us. Staying here was our only chance to live and he would not be driven from his ancestors and his village."

"You're telling me he was training you to help him fight this army of men?"

"Yes."

"And you went along with him! For god sakes Shelby you were only ten years old, how could he be so irresponsible." In the blink of an eye Shelby reached out and found the pressure point on the top of his right elbow. The pain was instant and paralyzing, even the breath was sucked from his lungs as he watched in slow motion as she leaned her face in close and whispered in a cold hard voice close to his ear.

"I loved him like a father, he pulled me from the depth's of a living hell and gave me a life of purpose, respect, strength and freedom, don't you ever voice disapproval of him in front of me." When Shelby released her touch on the Director he was so weak from the pain that he had to hold into the side of the table to stop from falling on his face. Shelby locked eyes with him as he tried to regain his composure before leaning back in her chair and closing her eyes. When she opened them again he was sitting up straight in his chair rubbing his elbow and staring at her. Shelby reached into her purse and pulled the F.B.I. identification out.

"I am truly sorry for losing control Director Daniels, you did not deserve that and I apologize. How I could have done that to someone I thank of as a friend---well, it was inexcusable. Please take these identifications and I promise I will be on the first flight tomorrow out of your wonderful country."

Director Daniels held the identification in his hands turning it over and over; finally he pushed back his chair and walked over beside her. He reached down and put the identification back in her open hand before softly kissing her on the top of her head.

"Take he to my hotel Agent Cruse, I need my sleep and we have a lot of work starting tomorrow."

Chapter 40

Alex and Vera stayed up late that night discussing the visit from Bill Mars. Vera wanted to call the authorities first thing in the morning; she did not like the answers Bill Mars had given them. The answers were all correct and said in the manner you would have expected a man in his position to give. But he was not interested in their company, not in the lease. She could see it in his eyes and the way he held himself while talking to them. One of the things she had to learn in law school was a persons posture and what it meant. The bells went off in her lawyer's head the moment he sat down and began talking, he was lying with every breath he took. She tried to convey to Alex her impression but he thought just the reverse, he liked the guy and thought he really was interested in buying the company. And as he said they had checked him out and he had the backing he needed to purchase the company.

"I don't know why were sitting here arguing about this Alex, were not going to sell the company now anyway. As soon as we go to the authorities and everything gets settled we can borrow the money from the bank and sell our interest in the other companies to pay back the sixty million. Let's go to bed Alex, I need something other than arguments from you right now anyway." Alex leaned over and gave Vera a long kiss before they stood and headed for the bedroom. But in the back of his mind he was working fast trying to think of something that he could say to change her mind. At lease not tomorrow, we can wait a couple of days, maybe even weeks before we have to do that. And he didn't for one second think Bill Mars was connected in anyway with the people she was talking about. Besides tomorrow is Saturday and the authorities aren't going to want to start an investigation on the weekend.

Bill Mars hung up the phone; the conversation was short with Jose Manual, *get me the information by tomorrow or my three associates will.* After talking to the Bell's for more than two and half-hours he had nothing more than what he had when he stepped off the plane. They were both very good at talking but not telling him anything and he knew if he didn't find something by tomorrow the Bell's would be in a world of hurt. He hated violence but sometimes it was necessary. Not that he would ever use his hands to hurt someone but there were always others that loved that job and were very good at it. He would snoop around their house tomorrow and talk to the neighbors you never know what you can pull from a snoopy neighbor.

The next morning Alex was out of the house by six and headed for his office. He had deliberately left early before Vera woke and began talking about going to the authorities. He had written a note telling her he had some work that needed to be completed today at the office and he would be back around six in the evening. That way he thought she would have no choice but to wait until next week to talk him into going down because he definitely was not going to the authorities on a Sunday.

Shelby was parked one block away sipping a steaming black cup of coffee when she saw him emerge from his house. It was time she talked to this Alex Bell, lay it on the line with him and find out just how involved he was. She turned the key as his car passed but before fully engaging the engine she saw the van pull away from the street and head in her direction. Easing back off the ignition she watch in her rear view mirror as the van approached and than passed her keeping the same speed as the Bell's car.

Two men in the front seats and one in the back and they weren't out for a Saturday drive to the coffee shop. She knew with the light traffic that she would be spotted if she tailed them. Instead Shelby made a left turn and headed for North West Expressway, this would take her downtown from another direction and if she goosed it a little she figured she could be close to his office and waiting for him when he arrived.

First Shelby thought, the Bell's get a visit from this Bill Mars, now he has three men tailing him on a Saturday morning. You had better watch your backside Mr. Bell because its getting ready to be put in a ringer and by the way he was driving she was sure he didn't have a clue that anyone was tailing him.

Shelby pulled into the bank parking lot a block away from his office and waited for fifteen minutes. When he never showed up she kicked herself, what made her think we was going to his office on a Saturday morning. Shit she thought why didn't I put a signal devise on his vehicles when I got to his house, now I don't have a clue where he went. Pulling out of the bank parking lot she headed down Broadway to catch the I-40 cross-town to get back to his house.

Less than a block down Broadway Shelby spotted the van and parked three spaces away was his car. Slowing down she scanned the buildings and was half-way passed the little coffee shop before she saw him standing in line to pay for his breakfast that he held in one hand. Finding a parking spot just a few spaces away Shelby locked the car and walked back toward the coffee shop on the other side of the street. Crossing the street a block from the shop she walked up behind the parked van and got a good look at two men sitting in the front seat. The back seat was empty which meant the third one must be close to Bell. Turning her head away as if she was looking in the glass windows she passed the van and walked up the steps to the coffee shop.

Alex Bell was sitting at a small round table beginning to eat his breakfast the third man was sitting against the wall in a booth that allowed him to look directly at Bell. Two other people were sipping coffee in another booth and no one looked up as she strolled to the counter and poured herself a cup of black coffee. After paying for the cup of coffee and before turning around she flipped the release strap holding the M11/9 Cobray that was held snugly by the pant suit she was wearing, just in case she needed to draw her weapon quickly.

Walking towards Alex Bell the third man made quick eye contact with her before turning his head and looking out the window. There was two empty seats at his table, should have been only one as there was elbowroom for only two people at the round table, Shelby took the one directly across from him manly because that position would keep the third man in view at all times.

She placed her cup of coffee on the table and was easing her self down to the chair when Alex looked up with a surprised expression on his face until she saw that he recognized her from yesterday on the elevator. Than his expression changed from surprise too curious.

"Good morning, I saw you yesterday on the elevator, are you following me?" Alex said with a smile.

"Your in deep shit Mr. Bell, your in way over your head." Shelby almost laughed when she saw the look, like the look of a deer caught in the beams of a fast approaching vehicle.

"What! I, I don't know what you mean, what are you trying------what are you-------who the hell are you anyway." The last part he said just a little to loud and all three customers looked in his direction. Shelby waited until all the heads turned back to what they were doing before saying anything. The third mans head also moved but so did his right hand as he slipped it next to his belt.

"I'm Agent Cruse, F.B.I. Mr. Bell," she said as she laid her documents on the table for him to see before putting them back in the left pocket of her jacket. "And as I said before your in deep shit, why don't you spend the next couple of minutes and tell me the full story, beginning at the point you got involved." Not once had Shelby mentioned the money or drugs or the dead man in the morgue, she waited for him to make his move, to see what he would do.

"Oh Christ! Vera was right I should have listened to her. Listen, listen please Agent Cruse we were going to, no! I mean we are going to turn in the money. Honest to god we were going to the authorities today as soon as I finish my work at the office. And we're going to pay back the sixty million we used to purchase those companies and the purchase of the notes at the bank just as soon as you guys said everything was done."

"You guys?"

"The authorities, you know the F.B.I. or the Drug Enforcement Agency, I don't know which one we just knew that's what we had to do! Uh, Uh, look I can show you everything we did and where the money is. I didn't spent a dime of it, not one dime."

"Not one dime? What was that you mentioned about some small change, sixty million wasn't it?"

"Well yeah, but I told you we were, no I mean we are going to pay it back, yes sir every penny of it." Shelby leaned in close and Alex automatically leaned in closer to her as she spoke.

"I want you to listen to me real good and do exactly what I tell you to do." Alex only nodded as he looked at her.

"When I tell you to I want you to act like your neck is sore and you turn your head to the right, God Damn it! I said wait until I tell you too. Alex half froze as he had begun to turn his head to his right. "Than I want you to turn your head to your left and as you do I want you to notice the single man in the booth with his back against the wall. Do not, I repeat do not look at him, just glance past as you flex your neck. If you understand nod your head. Ok, now do as I requested."

Shelby almost rolled her eyes while she watched him go through and exaggerated motion of what she had asked him to do, that really fooled anyone watching she thought as she shook her head.

"Do you know who that man is Mr. Bell?"

"No ma'am, I've never seen him before."

"That man has two partners outside waiting in a van and their job is to extract information from you in the most painful way they know how. Now reading up on you and your wife's life Mr. Bell I don't think you have any inkling of what pain is nor how some men inflict it on others with such pleasure." Shelby watched as small beads of sweat started popping out on his forehead.

"There working for the man you stole the money from Mr. Bell."

"Stolen! Hay I didn't steal any money from him, I found it, I found it while out jogging. Jesus Detective I was even trying to help the guy but he died anyway!"

"It's not detective."

"What!"

"I said it's not detective. I'm an Agent of the F.B.I. Mr. Bell."

"I'm, I'm sorry Agent Cruse, it's just that you got me rattled and I'm not thinking straight."

"Well Mr. Bell, you lean back and take a deep breath and than start from the beginning, if I think your telling me even one lie I'll get up and walk out of here and he can have his turn."

Alex couldn't help it, he took another quick look at the man who was pretending to be looking out the window before he started talking so fast that Shelby had to stop him a number of times to clarify a point. The recorder in her breast pocket took care of the details she would go over them later in her room.

An half hour later she had the whole story and he looked like he needed to go home and be tucked into bed, well she would leave that to his wife.

"Where are the keys to the locks for the five storage areas Mr. Bell."

"Right here." He said as he pulled from his pocket a set of keys. One loop had the five keys to the lock and he took them off and handed them all to her.

"Which one is to the lock on North Rockwell Ave unit?"

"I coded each one with a number. That was the last one so it should have a five scratched on it." Shelby found the key with the five scratched in it and took it off the key ring.

"Oh, by the way Mr. Bell if you actually counted the cash correctly as two billion, one hundred and seventeen million and you used sixty million, the count in each storage area would be four hundred eleven million, four hundred thousand. Not four hundred eleven million, two hundred thousand as you stated. You weren't planning on maybe keeping the extra two hundred thousand from all five storage areas for yourself were you?"

"What! No, no I gave you the keys all the money is there, every penny of it. What's going to happen now, to me and my wife?"

"I can't answer that Mr. Bell because I don't know. Go home to your wife and wait until another F.B.I. Agent contacts you."

"You're not going to put cuffs on me? I'm free to go home?"

"Like I said, go home to your wife and we'll be in contact. Finish your meal Mr. Bell and if you have real work you need to do at your office go ahead and do it, I'll be around." Shelby scooted the chair back making a loud ringing noise as she got up to leave. "Your lucky I found you first Mr. Bell rather than people like him." As she nodded towards the man in the corner who was now looking directly at her. She gave him a smile as she exited the coffee shop and walked down past the parked van. No one was in the van and not seeing them near by Shelby took a small square box from her purse, unscrewed the gas cap and dropped it in. five minutes after starting the vehicle the small box would expand cutting off the flow of gas to the motor. Walking down the other side of the street she crossed over and unlocked her car. Stripping off the jacket she pulled a loose fitting sweater over her shirt, placing her shoes in the trunk she slipped on a pair of rubber shoes that molded to her feet. Next she pulled a tight fitting pair of running pants from the bag in the trunk. Returning to her car she saw Alex Bell leaving the coffee shop with the man three steps behind. Looking around twice she finally spotted the two men from the van; they were in the alley half a block away from the van and in the location Alex was walking.

Getting in her car she took her time pulling her suit pants off and donning the running pants as she watched the action in her car mirror. By now Alex was running from the man following him but he was running directly to the other two men and when he came to the alley one of the men tackled him around the waist while the other slammed his fist against the side of his head. Alex went down in a heap and before he could gain his senses all three of them were carrying him to the van. One opened the side door while the other two threw him in and not very gently either. Ok, she thought, I got what I wanted to know about who they were.

This time they were in no hurry as they passed her car heading south towards the I-40 highway. Shelby started her car and slowly pulled out, keeping the van in sight, which was easy, as there was only two other cars ahead of her as they weave through downtown Oklahoma City. Shelby looked at the second's ticking off on the stopwatch incorporated into her regular watch she wore. She had punched it just as the van began to move down the street and the time read four minutes thirty-five seconds gone. As the van past the Carpenter Square Theatre Shelby watched as the van lurched two times before slowing and finally stopping.

Shelby pulled over to a parking meter some fifty yards from the van, got out of the car and waited. After trying to start the van for a few minutes the driver and passenger emerged and walked around to the sliding side door, the sliding door was now facing directly in front of her. As the men turned towards the sliding side door and began to open it she leaped, like a runner coming out of the starting blocks. The man in the van and Alex saw her coming as the man shouted to the two men who had their backs turned to her. When she reached them one of the men had gotten his hand to his gun but the other was turning to see who was coming. The palm of her left hand caught the turning man squarely on his nose and he died before his body hit the ground. Her right two fingers penetrated the spine at the small of the other mans back and for the remaining fourteen years of his life he would never walk again.

Turning to the remaining man inside the van she froze as two shots exited the roof of the van.

"That's right bitch, you just stay where you are or I'll put a bullet in his brain." He had one arm wrapped around Alex's neck and a gun in the other hand that was two inches from his temple. Sneering while he looked Shelby up and down a couple of times he finally said.

"You got some body pretty bitch, to bad I don't have the time or I'd show you what a real man could do to you."

He never saw the first hand coming before she flicked the gun away and crushed his hand. And when the second hand struck not only did he not see it he never saw anything else the rest of his life as two of the fingers on her left hand sunk one inch into each eye before pulling back and bringing the eye balls with them.

"Oh my God, oh my God you killed them you killed them!"

"Shut up Mr. Bell and come with me." Shelby said as she jerked him from the van and to her car. As she drove away she saw Bill Mars; eyes wide and mouth open staring at her through his windshield. Most of the way to his house he alternated crying and screaming about what she had done.

"F.B.I. Agents aren't suppose to do that, there not suppose to kill people in cold blood! For God sakes you ripped out the mans eyes, his eyes!" Shelby waited until he stopped his screaming before she spoke again.

"If I hadn't stopped them Mr. Bell in about an hour you would have been screaming a much different scream. They wouldn't have messed much with the niceties Alex, you would have been stripped naked and strapped to a wooden board where they would have attached electrodes to both testicles and a wire would have been inserted up your rectum. The current would than be turned on at a certain volume at which time you would make your first scream for mercy. Than they would show you the volume of the current, it would be on the lowest setting. They would do that so you would know the terrible pain you just felt was nothing to what you were going to feel."

"Looking at you Alex I would say they would know every thing they wanted to know in five minutes but the problem with torture is you can never be sure you have everything. So it would go on for a few more hours until your heart ruptured or gave out but each time the pain would get worse and you would know it was coming. Than Alex they would go after your wife and extract everything from her just to double their bet that they had gotten all the information. I won't tell you the things they would do to your wife Alex, but in the end she to would be dead."

"Get out of the car Alex and go to your wife, tell her everything than lock the doors and stay inside until the F.B.I. contacts you." Alex left the car a changed and frightened man.

Chapter 41

Quit a good start to the morning Shelby thought as she drove away from the Bell's resident. We have the money and we know who's in town and who's not. That will change as soon as she talks to Director Daniels and gives him most of the information. Hell it's only nine o'clock we might wrap this thing up tonight or tomorrow.

"Good morning Director, did you have a nice rest." Shelby said as she sat down in the dinning room at the Skirvin Hilton where Daniels was having his second cup of coffee.

"I did until I got a call from the local police chief at about seven-thirty this morning. Did that little mess outside the Carpenter Square Theater have anything to do with you?" Shelby shrugged her shoulders and gave Director Daniels a sweet girly smile all the while batting her eyes in extreme. He laughed out loud watching her pretending to be just a helpless little girl.

"I thought so, it looked like one of your operations. You frightened the hell out of the police chief, the three witnesses all described some superhuman woman stopping the van with her bare hands before ripping open the side door and killing all three men with only one strike of her hand. The witnesses also said one of the men shot this superhuman woman twice right in the chest and she never flinched."

Shelby sat straighter in the chair and pulled her jacket apart to look at her chest to see if there was any bullet holes in her.

"They must have been mistaken Director, my chest looks ok to me, don't you think?"

Director Daniels took a few quiet breaths with his eyes closed before looking up at Shelby and shaking his head slowly.

"You are in an awful good mood this morning Agent Cruse, care to tell me why?"

Shelby reached out with her hand and dangled a key change with four keys attached, the fifth key she had removed on the way to meet the Director.

"Would you like to know what these three keys open Director, you already know what the fourth key opens?"

"So we were right, the van carried a lot more than was in the first storage unit. Do you know how much money is there?"

"I haven't been there Director, I figured we could go together." Daniels eyes narrowed when she said she had not been there.

"Scout's honor Director." Shelby said as she raised two fingers in a scout's salute.

"Who was the man you rescued from the van this morning Shelby?"

"Just a frightened and broken man Director, he's not someone were interested in."

"Why don't you let me make that decision Shelby on whether he's important or not."

"Maybe later Director, right now we have big fish to catch. We both know the money came from Hector King and Jose Manual. They are the ones we want to see making a trip to Oklahoma City. And I think we have the man to get one of them here. His name is Bill Mars and Jose Manual hired him to find his money."

"Is this the man you helped this morning?"

"No Director, but he's the one with direct connections to Jose Manual and Jose is the only one that could get Hector King to the United States."

"What do we have to use against this Bill Mars to get him to defect to our side?"

"I'll tell him we'll feed his testicles to the fish while he watches, than I'll kill him."

"That's not funny Shelby, we don't feed people to the Piranha's in the United States. No matter how much we might like to, we have laws to take care of these kinds of people."

"Bullshit Jordan, you've let a man like Jose Manual reside in your country even with all the horrible things he's done through out the world. You call that good law, you've let him stay because you thought it was a good connection to Hector King. Fine Director, you talk to Bill Mars and see what comes of it and when you're done I'll talk to him, and I'll tell him how he's going to die if he doesn't cooperate."

"No Agent Cruse, you will not, you will follow the laws of this country, is that clear with you?"

"Yes sir!"

"Good, now lets check out the other three places he has the money stashed. If it's anywhere near the same amount the government is going to have one hell of a haul."

By that evening the money in all three areas were counted, the number handed to Director Daniels and Agent Cruse totaled one billion six hundred forty-five million six hundred thousand.

"I think the FBI's budget just got a little easier for agents to request new vehicles. Don't you think Agent Cruse? And thanks mostly to you for the sharp work you've done for us."

"Is that what the government will do with their big windfall, put it in with the rest of your budget and spend it on vehicle, maybe increased salaries for everyone also?"

"Hell it's better than letting the Federal Budget people get the money, at lease with us it won't be poured down a black hole that Congress seems to love to do with the trillions of dollars they spend each year."

"Couldn't the money be used for better things?"

"That's the system Shelby, get what you can when you can because if you don't the next agency will gladly take it away from you." Shelby turned away in disgust as the Director and two of his assistance started making up wish list for the future. Twenty minutes later he leaned down to the window of the car she had parked herself in when they started on their happy talk about where all that money was going.

"Ok Agent Cruse, tell me where we can find this Bill Mars."

Chapter 42

Bill Mars at that very moment was talking to Jose Manual about how one of his men had been killed. Bill did not do a very good job of describing the way the one man died and how the other two would never work for Jose again. Jose Manual continually interrupted him by saying he was describing things that no woman could do. Jose Manual finally told Bill Mars to park himself in front of the Bell's house and wait until someone else arrived to get the information from the Bells.

Hanging up the phone he just sat on the hotel bed reliving the memory of what he had witnessed this morning in downtown Oklahoma City. Even after telling Jose Manual about it everything still did not seem real. Bill had been the back up man for the three men that morning; his job was only to see that the men captured Bell than he was to call Manual. He had been sitting in his car almost a block down when he saw the woman opening the trunk of her car and start removing clothing in exchange for others she was putting on. Not only did it catch his eye because she was such a stunner but to see a woman undressing right beside her car was not the norm and not one with a gun strapped under her arm. When he saw her get in the car he started his car and drove down the street but a red light caught him and as he waited he glanced in his mirror and saw her pull out right after the van left. Without a doubt he knew she was following the van. When the light turned green he drove forward slow enough that both vehicles past him before turning right at the next light. Again the red light caught him but in Oklahoma he knew you could turn after stopping at a red light. This took only seconds but when he turned the first thing he saw was the woman running fast, faster than any person he had ever witnessed running. Running across the street towards the van that for some reason had stopped. He watched her movements, which were almost in a blur as she struck the two men outside the van almost instantaneously but when he heard the two shots he saw her jerk backwards before thrusting both arms into the van towards the man. He was sure the man had hit her at point blank range and he knew she was not wearing body armor, because he had watched what she had put on beside the car. But what really frightened him was the man stumbling from the van with black holes where his eyes should have been and an eyeball dangling down each cheek. If there weren't so much money involved he would have caught the next plane home.

Pulling up to the circular drive of the Sheraton Hotel in downtown Oklahoma City Director Daniels paused with his hand on the door handle and looked back at Shelby.

"We do this my way Agent Cruse, you stick with me, Agents Kelly, Mike you secure the hall on the sixth floor where he's staying." Showing his badge to the night manager he explained where they were going and that all elevator would be locked down except the one they were riding up on. No one was to take the stairs until he gave the all clear. The other two agents each took a separate staircase to the sixth floor and when they reached their destination each signaled their end of the hall was clear and secured.

Stepping in the elevator and pushing number six Director Daniels again repeated what he had said to her in the car.

"We will do this my way, you are not to speak to the man unless I give you permission!" Shelby looked straight ahead as if she was ignoring the Director. "God damn it Cruse do I have to send you back down on this elevator!"

"No Sir! Understood Sir!" Director Daniels watched her face all the way to six; there was no expression at all in her face. *If she runs from this elevator towards room sixty-seven by God I'll shot her in the leg.* When the elevator stopped he had his hand close to his gun but when it opened she didn't move until he walked out in front of her. Only then did she walk from the elevator a step behind.

With one agent on each side of the door Director Daniels took the hotel master key and inserted it into the slot. In a second the green light came on and he shoved at the same time he pushed the handle down.

Bill Mars still sitting on the edge of his bed heard the click of the lock and turned just as the door swung wide open. The momentum carried Director Daniels to the side of the room but gave Agent Cruse a direct line to the man and she took it.

The shock of seeing her bearing hard down on him and the murder he saw in her eye cause him to shout and fall backwards off of the bed at the same time Director Daniels shouted at Shelby. In two steps Shelby reached the man lying on his back, with his feet half way up the bed, and her fingers found the pressure point at the base of his skull. With the proper strength and skill you will instantly make the whole body tingle and than go numb. But the minute you release the pressure the effects are gone and that gave Shelby time to reach down and whisper in his ear.

"You answer his questions and do as he say's or I'll feed your eyes to the fish." In the same motion she lifted him up and placed him where he had been sitting before. To the three agents in the room it looked like she had rushed over and only helped him to the bed. Director Daniels had a relief look on his face for he thought he was going to have to confront her. A confrontation with Agent Cruse was not something he ever want to have but if it came to that he would, he just hoped he never had to.

Shelby stood slightly behind and above the Director as he pulled a chair over and began talking to Bill Mars who was still sitting on the bed with saucer like eyes. As the Director began questioning him, Bill Mars could not remove his eyes from Shelby's who was staring back without blinking. Even that scarred him about her she never blinked she didn't even move a muscle. *Everyone had to blink don't' they* he said to himself? Twice Director Daniels looked over his shoulders at Shelby before finally asking her to wait in the hall. With Bill Mars still looking at her she gave him a wide grin before turning and walking out the door.

A room was secured at the downtown Hilton by the F.B.I. for the interrogation of Bill Mars and within an hour Director Daniels, Agent Cruse and three additional F.B.I. agents took turns asking questions of Bill Mars. Shelby had insisted she be the first to question him and the Director reluctantly agreed but only because she was the one that found the players involved. Shelby had a good reason for wanting to be the first to question him, she wanted to get some facts on the table real quick, facts that Bill Mars understood was not to be questioned.

The room they secured at the Hilton was actually two rooms; one was a bedroom and the other a conference room. A table was in the center of the conference room with six chairs, all occupied with five facing Mr. Mars. Shelby started the interrogation as soon as Mars sat down in his chair, even before he was given the coke he requested.

"Mr. Mars I'm going to ask you a few questions and than I would like you to tell us about your relationship with Mr. Jose Manual." Mars started to open his mouth when Shelby leaned a little closer and said. "Mr. Mars I said I was going to ask you a few questions, you are to answer only those questions I ask of you so keep your mouth shut until than." Mars's mouth shut tight as he tried to lean a little further away from Shelby.

"We have the one billion six hundred forty-five million six hundred thousand dollars your boss tried to ship out of the country and we know he paid you five million to help him find the money. And to set the record straight, Director Daniels has the authority to charge you with the murder of one of your accomplice that was killed this morning."

"Me! You're the one that killed him not me!"

"Let me explain the United State Law to you Mr. Mars. It states that if anyone is killed in the act of a crime all accomplices may be charged with his/her murder. It is immaterial who or how the person is killed, do you grab what I telling you?" Mars only lowered his head and mumbled yes. She could see in his eyes when she mentioned the amount of money that he knew they had not found all of it and she also knew he was not going to mention that little error to them.

"Tell us how you are to contact Mr. Manual."

"I have a phone number and I am to call twice a day. The next call is to be at 11 P.M. tonight."

In the next hours Director Daniels and Shelby told him that when he called he was to tell Mr. Manual he had all his money but because it was so much he wanted Mr. Manual in Oklahoma City to pick it up. He also wanted his cut at that time. The meeting was to take place along the Oklahoma River at Wiley Post Park at Robinson and Southwest 17th street. The van would be parked next to the first playground after you entered the park. Director Daniels had picked this area because there were walking and jogging trails along both sides of the river and the area could hide a number of undercover officers doing a myriad of things. Another important point was the Oklahoma City Police Department had an Air Support Helicopter Unit at Western Avenue, less than a mile away that could lift off in thirty seconds if the call came to them.

After arguing with the Director for an hour Shelby convinced him that Hector King would never be drawn out of his country to meet with either Jose Manual, or Bill Mars whom he didn't even know. He would feel a trap because he was the one that had the money stolen in the first place. No, he would wait and find some other way to get his share of the money back.

When told what he had to do Bill Mars bulked, he wanted nothing to do with it, he would take his chances with the courts on the murder charges.

"At lease I'll be alive, if I go through with what you want me to do I'll have a very good chance of being killed!"

"What do you think I'll do to you Bill if you refuse?" Shelby said with a smile.

"That's enough Agent Cruse I guess I need to remind you once again you're a guest of the United States and you will obey our laws."

"She's not an F.B.I. Agent? She's not American?"

"She's been assigned to the F.B.I. so yes technically she's an F.B.I. Agent."

"Where is she from?"

"Colombia, She's a Drug Enforcement Agent for them."

"Oh shit! That was all he said as he looked between the Director and Shelby.

"The plan is a simple one Mr. Mars and you will be well protected the whole time your in the van." Shelby emphasized the word time to let him know he would be safe only if he did what they asked of him, if he didn't it wouldn't matter where he was or what jail or prison he was in she would get to him, and he knew it.

Chapter 43

Not convinced that Bill Mars had his money Jose Manual said he would send a trusted friend to verify. Bill Mars told him it was too big of a risk for him to show anyone but him the money and when he threatened to take his cut and leave the rest where it was and let him try and find it Manual changed his mind. He would meet him as planned.

Director Daniels and Shelby sat in an unmarked car at the top of the hill overlooking the Oklahoma River and the park less than a quarter mile away. They had arrived more than an hour ago and the time of the meeting was still two hours away. Director Daniels was sure Manual would be there early either to inspect the area or maybe hoping the van would already be there and he could surprise whoever was in the van and grab it before the meeting. Director Daniels and Shelby placed the small containers that held the Chinese food they had eaten in the sack and tossed it in the back seat. Sipping on a bottle of water Shelby asked the Director what he would be doing or going after today.

"You know the routine Shelby, the first thing I'll do is spend a god awful amount of time writing up the report and reading all the other agents reports before submitting it to the big guy. Than I don't know? I've got a vacation schedule but there could be another assignment for me when I return."

"What about you Shelby?"

"I'll be taking a vacation after I meet with someone."

"That someone wouldn't happen to be the old warrior, would it?" Shelby was silence for a minute or to before answering.

"No."

"I had a feeling you were going back to see him from the story you told me, so are you ever going to see him again?"

"No Jordan, I'm not going to see him again."

"Why Shelby, I know how much he means to you."

"He's dead."

"Oh! I'm sorry Shelby you never told me that in your stories, how did he die? I know you said he was in his late forties when he came to the village and he was there twenty some years when you came, did he die of old age or did he die fighting the men who came after him?"

Jordan almost instantly wished he had not asked her that question, for he could see it brought back painful memories and she was struggling to stay composed.

"That's Ok Shelby we don't need to talk about it, I'm sorry I brought it up." And he was sorry for he saw the turmoil running through her body, she wanted to talk and she wanted to be silent also but he saw her take a deep breath and say.

"I killed him."

"You killed him? You mean you couldn't protect him?" Her body began to shake as tears flowed down on her pantsuit. The sound started deep within her, the sound he had heard one other time on the pier at the Port of Catoosa. The sound she had told him was the death sound of an animal that knows it was about to die. He sat stunned as he watched her try and suppress the sound from flowing from her mouth but it kept coming until he felt the sound in the car would explode his eardrums. The sounds went to her very soul as she began to shake and sob even harder, and he did the only thing that he knew he should. He reached his arm around her and drew her body into his and held, held until the shaking and the tears dried up

With the color drained from her face and deep black holes for eyes she lay her head back on the headrest and closed her eyes.

"I killed him Jordan, I killed the one person that yanked me from hell, the one person I loved so much I would have died for. It's burned in my mind so deep and ugly it makes me sick when I think about that time.

He was teaching me how to direct all my energy to one object when I attacked a person and at the next instant redirecting that energy in another direction. He was teaching me so much and I felt like I was in the spirit world when he stopped in the middle of a sentence.

"They are here." Was all he said as he began walking back towards the village, I knew what he meant and the anger was so strong in me because men were coming to kill this man that only wanted to be left in peace. I vowed walking beside him I would die defending him. When we reached the small hill above the village we meditated the rest of that day and long into the night. At day break as we sat drinking the drink that would give us strength he pointed to the edge of the village where four men were emerging from the jungle. "

"As was the ritual each man stopped in front of the chiefs hut and laid a gift at his feet before turning in our direction. When I saw the four coming my anger so overwhelmed me that if the old warrior had not spoken harshly to me I would have ran down and fought them in the open. The jungle is our home and where our souls live, he said, they would guide us in this battle.

We wondered for five hours in the jungle and I thought maybe we were running away from the men but I also knew we had not tried to cover out tracks and would be easy to follow. So I was confused, why are we running instead of fighting and why are we leave tracks for them to follow? We completed a small circle and than a larger one in those five hours and when the Sun reached directly overhead he broke into a trot for another hour before suddenly stopping. The first man we saw was less than two hundred feet ahead of us following our trail. In another minute we had both found the other three slightly ahead of the first one. Without words I knew what the old warrior was going to do and also what I was to do. We split as he took the two on our left and I took the two on our right. Neither man saw the old warrior as he killed them, the first man did not see me before he died but the second man, a very large one, heard my attack and sidestepped the blow. He followed the path my body took and was bringing down his long knife when the old warrior struck him from behind. I would have died in that first battle if not for the old warrior, I had failed him and felt ashamed."

"For four more days they came, three, four and sometimes five at a time. Each day I improved my skills but more important I used my skills as he had taught me to use them. I no longer thought when the attacks came I reacted and blended to my surroundings. The last man on the fifth day was spotted by both of us coming down a steep ridge, by the time he was at the bottom of the ridge he was walking directly towards us. The old warrior was twenty feet in front of me and I thought he would make the kill but he let the man walk by less than two feet away. He was testing me, seeing if I could blend with nature as he had done. The fighter walked into my knife and was dead before he even knew I was two feet away."

"The next day four of them came, they were the last, you could tell by their skills for the best were always the last to come. For twenty-four hours they tracked us but the big advantage we had was that they always thought they were hunting one old warrior, they did not know of me. The following day I attacked one of them and before I killed him he had broken two fingers on my left hand and also my jaw. I watched as the old warrior waited for one of the men to enter his area and at the same time he was watching me coming close to another of the fighters. As I began my attack I spotted the last man coming from my side and I stopped my attack, but the old warrior could not see me by than. The old warrior saw him too and thought I did not. In his concern for me he tried to make his kill too quick and as the man was dying he kicked out and knocked the old warrior against a tree. His leg got caught in the vines around the tree. He went one way and his leg went another, when I got to him the femur in his right leg was splintered and sticking out his thigh."

"The two men were still coming in our direction and I knew I needed to get him out of there fast but he won't let me he said we would not make it, they were to close."

"This is hard for me Jordan, I don't let myself think about it, it's to painful."

"Than don't Shelby, sometimes things are better unsaid."

"Not this Jordan, not this I have needed to tell someone for a long time, I knew it the moment I started talking to you that first night that I would have to tell someone, I'm glad it's you."

"I asked him what he wanted me to do and he took his spear, placed the point on his heart. I knelt by his face and I cried to him that I couldn't do that but he said I had to. He said they would take his head and heart back to their land. That I must take his spirit into my own, I cried to him again that I couldn't do it but he grabbed my hand and put it on the spear. Hurry he said before they get here, it is what you were sent here to do for you are Tikwa and you must take my spirit into you, and than you will be the mighty Tikwa spirit."

Breathing heavy Shelby took two large gulps from the plastic water bottle before continuing.

"I could hear the fighters coming closer, they had not yet spotted us and he again whispered hurry, do not let my spirit leave my home. Than the old warrior smiled a smile of contentment and said, at last he could rest forever, as he closed his eyes. I shoved the spear through his heart as both men topped the hill, I do not have memories of the next few hours, I know I buried him deep in the jungle close to one of his favorite places for teaching me."

"What happened to the two men?"

"I have no memory of that but one of the young village girls that brought me food when I returned a week later said one lone man crawled to the village and told the story of a female fighter who had killed the old warrior. They had topped a hill and heard the screams of the dying coming from her throat as she pulled her spear from the old warrior. The man said she turned and ran up the hill where they were and she killed the man standing beside him with one blow to his neck before turning on him. He said she threw away her weapon and attacked him with her hands, each blow stopping just short of killing him. He said he knew she was killing him but she was doing it slowly as if she wanted to punish him forever and he said he would have died but for a black panther. When the blows stopped coming he turned his head and saw a large Black Panther growling at the woman and it was less than ten feet from her. But she was not afraid of the panther he could tell that, it was almost as if they were listening to each other, finally the woman walked away without looking back at him."

"He said he passed out and when he awoke it was morning but the Black Panther had not left, he had the feeling the animal had protected him throughout the night. For two days he stumbled and crawled to the village. Months later he was able to make it back to the land where he came from and the legend of Tikwa was born, more powerful than the old warrior's."

"But you never stayed there you were found I can guess, a few months later wondering into the town of the people who adopted you."

"Yes, I left a few weeks after that, I had to find a better life, there was nothing left there for me. I'm sorry I lost control Jordan, thank you for your silence and support. Many times I feel like I don't belong to the normal human race but I know I'm at peace in the jungle and that bothers me."

"The normal human race! Look around you Shelby, who's normal I know I'm sure as hell not, not even the guy flipping hamburgers at McDonalds. Were made by our experience Shelby and we learn to survive the best we can it's just that some of us have a much harder life than others can ever imagine. I couldn't begin to think how or what I would be if I had the experience you did as a child. I know your one hell of an agent, most would say the best ever and if it wasn't for your child hood I don't think you would have been. So remember we are all forged from the life that was given to us."

"You didn't mention I am also a skilled cold bloody killer."

"That just makes my point Shelby, look at your childhood, you either adapted like you did under the circumstance or you died, you choose to live as most everyone else would. Quit beating yourself up, let it go Shelby and start being happy with yourself and for God sake get laid sometime, it will do wonders for your ego."

They both started laughing at that and almost didn't hear the radio.

Chapter 44

"Shit! The truck's moving, who's in the truck with Mars?"

"Block it at the entrance! Block it at the entrance damn it." One agent managed to get his vehicle sideways of the entrance seconds before the big van roared across the lawn and took the second exit where no one had yet gotten too. Hitting Robinson Avenue the big van fished tailed twice before straightening up and started south with three vehicles coming hard out of the park. Director Daniels and Shelby were in the fourth car and were still in the upper part of the park when the big explosion happened, right in the middle of the three agency vehicles. The Director's car was hit with a large piece of metal squarely on the windshield causing him to lose control and hit the playground equipment in the middle of the park.

Director Daniels had called for the helicopter backup as soon as he saw the truck roaring out of the park and it was already in the air. Within three minutes the report came back that the truck was spotted pulling into one of the abandoned warehouses seven blocks south.

Ordering that the helicopter stay above the warehouse Director Daniels regrouped his team, minus the six dead and wounded agents in the three cars, and surrounded the warehouse. For one hour the Director tried to negotiate but no answers came back through the door of the building. Finally the Director ordered the door to be blown off and an F.B.I. Swat team stormed in. when the battle was over Jose Manual and the one man that came with him was dead. Bill Mars sitting in the van had been surprised and had been killed by a silencer, by Jose Manual while still at the park.

Monday morning while Alex and Vera were still sleeping a visitor entered their house and confronted them, when the visitor left a key chain with one key dangling from it was in the palm of Vera's hand. At three o'clock in the afternoon Director Daniels was parked in a no parking zone at the Oklahoma City International Airport waiting for Shelby to finish checking in for her flight to New York and on to Colombia. Watching her walk back towards the car the director was sad and happy at the same time. She was a beautiful woman that he would have liked to get to know her much better, but with her baggage he was happy to see her leaving his country. What a paradox he thought, she looks so beautiful on the outside but on the inside was a dark cold pit and she was dying.

"Got everything, thanks for clearing the channels so quick Jordan."

"My pleasure Agent Cruse, are you going back to working in the field in Colombia?"

"No Jordan, I have an old friend I must find to give some information to and by than the crops will have been harvested and they will be coming."

"They will be coming? What, who will be coming Shelby."

"The seekers of glory Jordan."

"The seekers of glory! What are you talking about Shel--------Oh sweet Mary of Jesus Shelby, No! You can't start that up again, you have to forget it you have to get on with your life!"

"That is my life Jordan."

"Please Shelby stay here, let the doctors help you through this, don't start it up again."

"I'm not starting it up again Jordan, it never stopped."

"It never stopped? How could it not stop, who could have fought them Shelby, your said yourself they were after the glory of killing the great spirit, knowing it would make them heroes in their land for the rest of their lives and even believing it will help them in the next world. You said the old warrior wanted his spirit to stay in his jungle with you!"

Director Daniels did not realize he had reached for her hand when he started talking to her and now with her hand in both of his he looked into her eyes. He saw the truth and the sadness as she smiled at him.

"Thank you Jordan I will always remember you with friendship and love."

"You went back! Every five years you went back why?"

"Because that is my destiny Jordan, it has been my destiny from the day I was born, please understand."

"I, I can't Shelby, I can't understand that, nothing is stopping you from staying here."

"That is my home Jordan, that is where I feel free and at peace." Shelby opened the door and slid out, when she closed the door she looked in the open window and smiled a million-dollar smile at him.

"Jordan Daniels you make a woman go weak in the knees, if I ever get my head on straight you had better watch out because I will be coming to find that lay you talked about." He watched her back until she disappeared through the door, not once did she look back.

Chapter 45

Deep in the Colombia jungle Shelby squatted watching the trail ahead as she adjusted the gag on the mule lying by her feet. Two hours ago he had trudged down this trail carrying the money from the last drug sell, the money belonged to Hector King. Shelby was waiting for the man who was sent to collect and return the money to the large white house on the hill.

Landing in Bogota, Colombia Shelby was met by Director Ruiz who handed her a sheet of paper with the address of the man's name she had fax him earlier.

"You won't be coming back to work with me will you Agent Cruse."

"No Captain, sorry old habit, no Director I won't be coming back, I will miss you."

With the address in hand Shelby was now waiting for the man who's name was on the sheet of paper. She had little time to wait, she heard him before she saw him coming around the small bend. There was a full moon and she saw his face as he approached, she smiled for she would have recognized him even after twenty-two years. As the man stepped out into the small clearing to wait for his mule he looked at his watch and frowned. The man should have been here by now, he thought, if anything has happened he would have hell to pay when he reported it to his boss, Hector King.

Shelby waited and watched the man for a minute before going back twenty-two years to that terrible black day. He had asked her if she had seen his father and she lied to him, she had been afraid of saying anything, afraid of telling her friend, Jesus Garrido that his dad had been taken to the big house on the hill, She shrugged the thought away and moved.

Shelby swiftly took the rifle from his hand before he knew it was gone.

"Hello Jesus, it's been a long time."

"Where did you come from, what do you want with me I'm just a poor labor trying to make a living, I don't have any money."

"Relax Jesus, I don't want your money, although you lie to me, you have a lot of money." Shelby said with a broad smile. Jesus squinted to get a better look at the woman talking to him who also knew his name.

"I don't know you? How do you know my name?"

"Little Jesus Garrido, don't you recognize me?"

"I'm not sure, you do look familiar but I can't put a name to you."

"You said I could talk to the animals and understand them also." Looking at her hard Shelby watched as his memory tried to bring up things long forgotten and than she saw the recognition dawn on his face and she smiled again.

"Shelby the Mustang!" That was the name he always teased her with. Lying the rifle down she reached out and hugged him tight.

"Shelby, but you died when you were nine! They said by the same man that killed your mother."

"They tried Jesus, they tried very hard but they lost. Walking over to the bush she reached down and pulled the man up that she had tied and gagged. Untying him and pulling the gag off she told him to run down the trail and don't look back before he reached his home. Than she told him to stop as she reached down and pulled a packet of money from the pack. She stuffed the money in his pocket, more money than he would make in ten years before again telling him to run home to his family and get out of this business. Jesus watched and said nothing until the man was gone.

"I will be in very deep trouble if I don't take the full amount of money to Mr. King Shelby, why did you do that?"

"Because I have something to tell you Jesus and than you must make a decision, a decision that I will not stop you from doing which ever way you choose. If you choose one way you will solve the problem if you choose the other I will solve the problem."

For the next half-hour Shelby told Jesus about his father's death and how she witnessed it and about what happened to her.

"You live in the big house now Jesus, have you ever came across a blue door on the lower level, just before the hall makes a sharp right turn."

"Yes I have seen this door, but no one is allow to open it or go down to the next level except for Mr. King and two other men."

"That is the door to the marble stairs that lead to the two pools Jesus, the pool that your and my father died a horrible death in. When you go back to the big house check out what I have told you. You have a choice Jesus you may take this money and run to a big city where you will be safe or you can give him the same kind of death he gave our fathers."

"I have wondered for many years about my father, I always felt King killed him but he took me in and gave me shelter when my father did not come back. I will check out what you have said Shelby and if I find the pool than I promise you and our fathers I will kill him in the same way."

Shelby reached down and handed the money to Jesus but he refused it.

"I don't want his dirty money, you take it."

"No Jesus, you take it and make a life for yourself afterwards, the money is not dirty only him. Jesus when you contact Mr. King use the word Archaic. With that word he will trust you completely and you can use that trust to get him to the pool. Someone else used that word to help him escape when someone was trying to kill him a few months back. "

"Shelby watched as he shifted the money to his backpack than turning he hugged her and thanks her for coming and telling him. As he started to leave Shelby took a small packet from her backpack and handed it to him.

"Its plastic explosives Jesus, a little will go a long way, when you finish put equal amounts across the back and the complete compound will slide down the hill."

Chapter 46

On the third page of the financial section of the Oklahoman newspaper a few weeks later readers noted a short article that gave this information. Mr. and Mrs. Alex and Vera Bell of Oklahoma City sold the WittBell company that they starter from scratch more than twenty years ago. In an interview with this newspaper they stated that they had been thinking for a long time how to help the young people who had gotten involved in drugs and specially those that have been or are in prison. They have formed a not for profit organization that will start building medical facilities across our great state. There will be no charge for any patient that is accepted into the program. The program not only helps each individual to escape the terrible cycle of drugs but also how to live and function as a productive citizen. When asked how much it would cost the Bell's only answer was, what ever it takes. The rumor mill in the financial community was that they would fund between four hundred million and four hundred fifty million dollars for the project. The only comment this reported can think of is that this is the way it should have been done all along. Our prisons are filled to capacity and sixty-five to seventy percent are in prison because of drugs or drug related crimes. God will bless the Bells for such a great gift to our state was the way the reported ended the piece.

As the first rays of the sun peaked down on the village Shelby watched from the jungles edge as the first four slowly emerged from the jungle and made their way to the chief's hut where they left their gifts. She was at peace and she felt the sprit of the old warrior smiling down on her. She felt the freedom of the wind caress her face as she formed and reformed the shape of her hands. I am home she sighed as she closed her eyes in preparation.